OUT ON A LIMB

OUT ON A LIMB

Sue Limb

With illustrations by Ros Asquith

This first hardcover edition published in Great Britain 1999 by
SEVERN HOUSE PUBLISHERS LTD of
9–15 High Street, Sutton, Surrey SM1 1DF.
Originally published in Great Britain in 1992 in paperback format only.
First published in the USA 1999 by
SEVERN HOUSE PUBLISHERS INC., of
595 Madison Avenue, New York, NY 10022.

British Library Cataloguing in Publication Data
Limb, Sue, 1946-
    Out on a limb
    1. Love stories
    1. Title
    828.9'14'08 [F]

    ISBN 0-7278-2292-6

Printed and bound in Great Britain by
MPG Books Ltd, Bodmin, Cornwall.

Having your photo taken

When I was about thirty,
I noticed something odd.
When not smiling, my face
took on a collapsed and
tragic look. If it didn't
actually swash, it buckled.
The camera started to
suggest I was sad and
haggard whereas I knew
very well I was relaxed and
serene – well, as relaxed and
serene as one can ever be in
the late twentieth century.

God, I'm exhausted. I've just had my photograph taken. Not a casual holiday snapshot with the pigeons of St Mark's on my head and an out-of-focus ice-cream seller walking across the foreground – unfortunately. This was the real thing. The endless focusing while your smile runs away down your shirt front. The photograph for (oh dear!) Professional Purposes – this page in fact. Twenty-four exposures. I almost died of exposure, there and then.

There I was: backed up against the Venetian blind, my heart sinking with every click of the shutter. It sank right down into my boots, which, God knows, were tight enough before. Suddenly, standing up didn't seem so easy any more. How, in heaven's name, had I managed it all these years? My knees buckled and my whole frame wavered ominously like one of those industrial chimneys which has just been dynamited and teeters on the brink of brickdust.

And what on earth was I supposed to do with my hands? Up till now I'd had no trouble with them. We'd had some good times together, me and my hands. Many's the delicious canapé they've smuggled to my lips over the decades. They'd been most cooperative in the past. But one click of the shutter and they seemed to have lost their nerve.

My left hand had seized a fistful of buttock (my own, fortunately) and was squeezing it with a fervour I had not experienced since a certain Neapolitan sailor. My right hand was slithering menacingly up my lapel, towards my neck. Yes, it was *grasping my windpipe*. What was going on? Was I about to throttle myself to death – *on camera*?

'Relax,' said the photographer, snapping away like a

piranha at my shrinking flesh. Now, I've always had trouble with this word *relax*. I think I know what it means, in theory, but I regard it as a kind of transcendental, blessed state to which a nail-biting, finger-picking, buttock-squeezing mortal like myself can never aspire.

I did try to relax, once, in 1972 I think it was, but to be honest I found it damned hard work. And on this present occasion I could no more relax than escape backwards into another dimension through the Venetian blind, filleting myself in the process.

I longed for a paper bag into which to thrust my head. I wouldn't have minded so much if it was mere *torso* the camera was after, the shoulders downwards faithfully recorded, the head poignantly missing, like some antique statue. My mother's taken hundreds of photographs like that, over the years. I used to think it was incompetence, but now I realise it was kindness.

I haven't always cringed from the camera. The photos of me aged eight are a great success. A perfectly normal little boy grins out of the past with his shorts and short-back-and-sides. 'Call me Norman,' I told my mother, who responded by calling me something else entirely. But still I climbed trees, played cricket and read prisoner-of-war stories. And I Smiled Please with effortless ease.

But the time comes when a boy has to put away childish things and devote his attention to the perverse business of becoming a woman. The adolescent photos all show clearly that things have started to go wrong. My body, suddenly out of control, has started its journey towards matronliness. The Brando scowl, pugnacious fists and carelessly sprawling knees hint at the torment within.

'Where's my stubble?' the dark eyes seem to wonder. 'What's this goddamn bosom thing hanging around my neck?'

A few years on, and my capitulation to femininity was complete. It was the era of mini-skirts and face paints. I leer out of my late Sixties mug shots through a kaleidoscopic haze of blusher, glitter and gloss. Earrings were big, then: I had a pair of snakes, a pair of parrots and a pair of pigs. There was hardly a member of the animal kingdom that had not dangled from my lobes. At times I resembled nothing so much as a recently decorated abattoir.

So the little boy grew up to be a female impersonator. These photographs now embarrass me, but my recently acquired husband loves them – the shameless young floozy he never knew flaunts herself at him from the wall of his studio. I don't know whether to scratch her eyes out or be glad that his Other Woman is still, somehow, me. Or is she? They say the camera cannot lie, but the longer I live, the more preposterous its untruths seem.

When I was about thirty, I noticed something odd. When not smiling, my face took on a collapsed and tragic look. If it didn't actually swash, it buckled. The camera started to suggest I was sad and haggard whereas I knew very well I was relaxed and serene – well, as relaxed and serene as one can ever be in the late twentieth century.

Pretty soon lines were spreading over my face like a history of the railways. Time's wingèd chariot had skidded right across my cheeks – you could see the wheel-ruts – and if I smiled, they deepened into ravines. If I didn't, the photograph would look like a Wanted For Terrorism poster.

After you're thirty, what the camera wants from you is bones. Virginia Woolf had wonderful cheekbones and eyesockets, and even so she appears wisely to be hiding behind children and hats in the snapshots taken of her on windy beaches. Being neither upper class nor remotely Jewish (even by marriage) I could offer no bones to the ravening lens. All I threw it, facially speaking, was a bun that was past its best.

So nowadays I try and make sure I'm safely *behind* the camera, with my finger on the trigger – I mean, button. And as the accursed paparazzi poke their zoom lenses out from behind a sheltering palm tree, hoping to snatch a glimpse of a royal torso, even so do I stalk my prey: my baby daughter.

Babies, I find, don't know what the camera is and are sublimely indifferent to its greedy eye. No wonder they all look so delicious. I'm hoping that old age – if I get that far – will bestow the same indifference. By then my façade will be as craggy as a remote Cornish cliff, with guillemots nesting in the gullies. I shall regard the camera with the serene tolerance offered by an Ancient Monument and, with a September sunset streaming across my West Front, I hope once more to achieve some measure of the picturesque.

Having a bad memory

I was introduced recently to
Kenneth Longbottom.

'Hello, Kenneth,' I smiled,
and even as I spoke his
hindquarters drooped
elegantly downwards
until they dragged along
the floor behind him
like a peacock's tail.

'Who's that?' hissed somebody in my ear.

'Keith Endless-Ass,'
I stammered.

My memory has never been my strong point. Some people seem to remember things in frightening detail. How do they do it? And even more puzzling, why? A chap came up to me at the theatre the other night and I had to admit that his face was familiar. Was he, perhaps, the milkman? The postman? A bit-part actor in a cough linctus ad? He seized me by the sleeve, his face alight with recognition. Maybe I was *his* milkman?

'Sue!' he cried – rather disturbingly, without a moment's hesitation.

'Hey!' I faltered. 'Hello! What are you doing these days?'

'Oh, the same as ever,' he shrugged, infuriatingly refusing all clues. And then he told me what a wonderful time we'd had back in the summer of 1973 (or was it 1773?) when he'd played third palace guard in my never-to-be-remembered amateur production of that play (what's it called? – the one with the lion in it).

'Remember the cast party after the last night?' he leered. 'You were really on form, eh? Nudge, nudge, wink, wink.'

It's galling enough, I feel, to behave badly, without being *reminded* of it.

Nowadays parties are passé, thank goodness, and I devote all my energies to a little gardening. But even that's an absolute minefield.

'What's that dainty little plant?' asked my friend Eve yesterday. We were strolling in the shady part of the garden where my white form of love-lies-bleeding was dangling its elegant petals in the breeze. No, I tell a lie. It's bleeding heart. Colloquially. Or am I thinking of love-in-idleness?

'Anyway,' I said, 'in Latin it's, you know, whatyoumacallit Alba.'

'Bernarda Alba?'

'No, no, she was someone else. Or am I thinking of that Duke of Alba who ruled the Netherlands in the sixteenth century?'

'The only other Alba I know is a town in Provence.'

'No, that's Albi.'

'No, that's the other town.'

'What on earth is it, then?'

There was a pause in which the slow grinding of brains could be heard.

'*Dicentra spectabilis Alba!*' I cried in triumph – but by then it was the middle of the night, two weeks later.

'Bless you!' mumbled my sleeping spouse.

'I must remember to send Eve a card with *Dicentra spectabilis Alba* on it,' I thought. But I forgot.

If it's like this when you're barely forty, what hope is there for memory at sixty? It's not just the Latin names of flowers, which, God knows, are best forgotten anyway. (Although I have a soft spot for *Arabis Fernandii-Coburgii Variegata* – it sounds like an illegitimate princeling from way back along the Victoria line.)

No, I have problems with people's names, too. Especially my old schoolfriends' married names. If pressed, I substitute them for a slight cough.

'This is Lorna Ahem,' I murmur. 'Janet Er-er's cousin – you remember?', and I glide away into the nearest crowd.

I also find it impossible to remember if my friends know each other. I have lived in several different corners of the country and made new friends each time, and been visited by them (boy, have I been visited by them – but that's another story). Sometimes several have visited at once.

'Have you met my friend Janet Er-er?' I asked What's-his-name recently. 'Met her?' he exclaimed. 'We were married for five years. You came to the wedding. Don't you remember?'

The solubility of marriages these days doesn't help. They fizz for a few minutes, like those giant vitamin C pills, and then vanish for ever, leaving only flatulence and heartburn.

My most appalling sin, though, is forgetting appointments.

11

I'm supposed to write them on the calendar, immediately. But there are four phones in our house, and only one is by the calendar. If the calendar isn't handy, I write appointments on old bus tickets or the sole of my shoe. Thinking *I won't forget that in a hurry.* And indeed I do often forget things slowly and gradually, which I suppose is a hopeful sign. But when the phone rang a few weeks ago and Janet Er-er said, 'We were sorry not to see you last night,' my blood turned to ice and I felt my life spiralling out of my control. I rushed out and bought three more calendars, one for each phone. (Too bad I always forget to collate them.)

I've started making emergency arrangements to remember people's names, too. Like the tricks employed by the old Roman orators – what were they called? – mnemonics? (Or is he a Czech dissident?) When introduced to somebody, you make a visual picture of his name and project it on to him. I was introduced recently to Kenneth Longbottom.

'Hello, Kenneth,' I smiled, and even as I spoke his hind-quarters drooped elegantly downwards until they dragged along the floor behind him like a peacock's tail.

'Who's that?' hissed somebody in my ear.

'Keith Endless-Ass,' I stammered.

'Not one of the Endless-Asses of Hertfordshire?' she asked.

I panicked. I couldn't remember whether Hertfordshire was Herefordshire or not.

The anguish of failing memory is becoming so acute that I am taking to drink. Not much drink. Always having teetered on the brink of teetotalism, all I need is an acorn-cupful of Beaumes de Venise and I'm on my way – like some disreputable little creature from Beatrix Potter. Wine brings forgetfulness, so I bask in its warmth, grateful to be able to forget that I forget.

As for the flowers – who cares? Wandering among their glowing colours and exquisite scent, feeling their velvety leaves and watching the bees cuddle into them, I feel gloriously drunk on the beauty of the natural world even without my acorn cup of Beaumes de Whossname. Why give flowers names, in any case? I'm sure it was his idea. You know who I mean. What's-his-name, back in the Garden of Edam. I think it begins with an A.

Phobias

When it comes to going slightly round the bend (and it comes to us all at some time or another) the two most popular forms are apparently obsession and phobia. Obsessive people get up in the night to switch the light on and off to make sure it's working. Phobic people never dare to touch the switch without wearing gloves and rubber boots.

I've always preferred phobias myself. Much more romantic. There's something awfully fiddling and mundane about obsessional behaviour. But develop a phobia and life transmutes into a heroic key: death, shame and destruction lurk around every corner, and only the most desperate courage can get you through that ride in the lift or past that silently poised spider.

I don't like to boast, but I've had some epic phobias in my time. Claustrophobia was an early favourite. Wherever I was, I had to sit near the door. Preferably with part of my leg already around it, toes poised in the fresh air ready to escape. This caused a certain amount of trouble in crowded restaurants and dark cinemas, but I still clung tenaciously to any available door, despite, at times, quite frenzied competition.

There are lots of us clawing our way towards the slightest hint of a chink, you know. In fact, I'm sure I speak for all claustrophobics when I way that there aren't nearly enough doors to go round. How measly of architects to bestow one solitary door on the average room. Why not two? Why not twenty? When faced with a shortage, the sufferers usually install themselves within easy leap of a window – unless, of course, they're on the seventh floor. And then – oh, the reeling of the brain and the screeching of the toenails as one has to choose between claustrophobia and fear of heights.

I suppose behind all phobias is a fear of death – silly, really, since death's the last thing we should worry about. At college I rushed down to my tutor one evening, flung her door open and cried,

'I'm sorry to disturb you, but I think I'm going to die!'

'I'm sorry to hear that, Sue,' she murmured. 'Will you have time for a glass of sherry first?'

It was at college that I decided to specialise, and developed nauseaphobia. It's fear of being sick – but, in my case, particularly of doing so in public. At home it would've been all right, though I wouldn't have wanted the television to be *actually watching me*, if you know what I mean. Formal public occasions were the worst: the Lord Mayor's banquet, the supermarket queue. It's amazing how quickly you can start feeling sick if you put your mind to it, and how quickly it vanishes once you're restored to fresh air and solitude.

In time my phobia got bored and moved on. I don't need so much fresh air and solitude these days. Just as well, as there doesn't seem to be so much of it about.

But guess what: a brand-new phobia seems, after all these years, to be creeping up on me. *Choking to death in public.* You'd think if I had to go through this wretched phobia business again, it could at least be something new. Fear of tennis racquets, maybe. Or paint brushes. But no. There I was last week, grabbing a quick lunch between business appointments, glad to have found a chic little vegetarian restaurant, when it struck. A strand of cress got caught on the edge of the abyss. You know the abyss. The one right at the back of your tongue.

I went hot. I went cold. Goose pimples fled across my skin. *This is it*, I thought. *I'm choking to death. Here and now, in this not very distinguished restaurant. And alone. Not even a friend on hand to stand over my still-twitching corpse and say*, 'Ladies and gentlemen, history will reveal that she was quite a dignified person normally.'

The cress trembled on my tonsils: the Grim Reaper loomed up, steaming out of a vat of ratatouille, and leered in my direction. With a heroic effort, I produced from some mysterious part of my body the kind of blow normally only associated with industrial vacuum-cleaners in reverse. Somehow (and I take this as evidence that there must be a God after all) the cress ended up immobilised between my lips. Insolent little strand of weed! I wanted to kill it – as inhumanely as possible. Unfortunately it was already dead so I spat it at the Grim Reaper and he disappeared in a puff of pastry with cream cheese and spinach.

Spinach. That's another tonsil-tangler. Now that I'm clearly going to choke to death, suddenly all the vegetables in the world are fighting for the chance to do the deed. The hard-hearted artichoke is still current favourite, but I notice that the skins of tomatoes are turning into PVC and what used to be celery is now little more than a moist noose.

Vegetables aren't the only villains, though. Meat lurks murderously on its slab, its sinews coiled and ready to unfurl and lasso my larynx. As for carbohydrate, there is nothing more fatal than the kamikaze crumb that will zoom unerringly down your windpipe, flying into the eye of the storm.

The only safe food, I've decided, is consommé. Though how much consommé would you need to actually drown in the stuff? Would one greedy slurp be enough, if it went down the wrong way? Maybe I should start taking consommé straight into the vein.

They do say that talking about your phobia will cure it. And yes, even as I write this, I'm beginning to feel better. My gorge is sinking. I think I could manage something solid now. Even something stringy. Celery, maybe. In fact, I'm feeling ravenous. Damn celery – bring me something *really* stringy. A harpsichord! The Bayeux tapestry! Elgar's Introduction and Allegro for Strings!

I think that's got rid of that phobia. Perhaps I do fancy an obsession after all. It won't be light switches, though. It'll be Charles Dance.

Going to the loo

Have you noticed how each nation has its own unique loos? The nihilistic French, for example, sometimes offer little more than a couple of footplates and an abyss. But at least an abyss is the right principle. The Germans, bourgeois and acquisitive in their loo design if nothing else, provide something unpleasantly like a mantelpiece. Now, I'm not averse to mantelpieces, but I do prefer them to be at eye level, adorned with potpourris and ormolu clocks.

I've just had That Dream. You know: the Looking-For-The-Lavatory dream. And this one was the worst ever. Because it started so well: it bid fair, indeed, to be the dream of my wildest dreams. There I was at the National Theatre, hobnobbing with Peter Hall (or was it Albert?) and watching a rehearsal of a play *I'd written*. What heaven! But then I realised I wanted to go to the loo – something people in heaven don't have to bother with at all.

Even when one's wide awake, finding a loo on the South Bank can be tough. When you're asleep, it's impossible.

'That'll be £1 for the proper loo!' insisted a grim-faced attendant, shaking a collecting box.

'£1? Disgraceful!' I cried, and ran off to the improper loos. They turned out to be a row of fishtanks, in which several customers were already comfortably installed, with water up to their armpits, chatting amiably. Horrors!

I ran on, passing loos of unspeakable foulness, loos without walls or doors, loos that turned into piano stools and washbasins before my very eyes.

'Oh please!' I panted, buttonholing a motherly woman, 'Here's a pound! Where's the proper loo?'

She led me swiftly to what looked like a high-tech potty, and I threw myself upon it . . . only to discover that I was seated in the middle of the Olivier stage, with hundreds of theatregoers smiling at my humiliation.

I suppose your subconscious refuses to provide you with a suitable loo in your dreams so you'll wake up in time to go to the real one. All the same, is all this torment really necessary? Or is it part of Civilisation and Its Discontents, about which old Sigmund warned us? I bet baboons don't have Looking-For-The-Lavatory dreams.

Perhaps I'm peculiarly inhibited, but I have a fair bit of lavatory angst even in real life. I'm only really happy on my very own loo. In fact, whenever I move house, I always want to uproot the loo and take it with me. Other people's loos make me feel uneasy, somehow: one has to steel oneself to face the alien ballcock.

I know a family whose house is built around the loo. Every room radiates from it, and something about the acoustics ensures that even a discreet cough therein rolls around the entire establishment like a clap of thunder. Luckily they live near a park, which has the perfect public loo: dark, deserted and storm-tossed. When I am staying, I wing my way thither several times a day, crying *'Time for my jog round the park!'*

While we're on the subject (and yes, I'm afraid we still are) have you noticed how each nation has its own unique loos? The nihilistic French, for example, sometimes offer little more than a couple of footplates and an abyss. But at least an abyss is the right principle. The Germans, bourgeois and acquisitive in their loo design if nothing else, provide something unpleasantly like a mantelpiece. Now, I'm not averse to mantelpieces, but I do prefer them to be at eye level, adorned with pot-pourris and ormolu clocks.

Foreign loos also hide behind totally confusing names. In Italy, for example, you will be faced with a crisis of identity: are you SIGNORE or SIGNORI? If you wait long enough, you should see a person of identifiable sex or other (terribly old-fashioned, the Italians) either emerging or converging. Greek loos, I found, were even more mysterious. There were two doors, even in a remote hillside loo: one for Us and one for Them. But which was us? GAENOKALYPTIKI? Or ANTHRAXAZPIRIN? Both offered a hole in the ground – equality of a sort, I suppose, though I'd always hoped equality would be a question of levelling up.

But at least the Greeks offered a loo of sorts. I sometimes think my troubles stem from a school trip to Belgium where there seemed to be no public loos at all. No wonder they call it Gallant Little Belgium. Our coach rolled ever southwards, but the magic sign DAMES did not appear. Our girlish songs ceased, and the uneasy silence was only punctuated by screams whenever the bus jolted over a rut.

Eventually we came to a wood, and the driver pulled up. All my schoolmates scuttled out and sought relief among the hazel copses, but somehow, agonised though I was, I couldn't. I had to be the immaculate exception. I sat it out with the grown-ups, didn't I, keeping a stiff upper lap.

It was another one and a half hours before we reached our hotel, by which time I had turned to stone. I resembled nothing so much as a statue of Queen Victoria – unyielding granite; and very regal. And when at last I came to the throne, I reigned for what seemed like sixty-three years.

All this anguish hints at some profound psychological damage, don't you think? Has my potty training actually driven me . . . potty? All those years ago, my mother beamed approvingly at me on my plastic throne, but was I really sitting on a time bomb?

Does everybody feel this way? My husband tells me that men don't have Looking-For-The-Lavatory dreams. I suppose that's true. After all, Jacob's slumbers were enlivened by visions of his Ladder, not his bladder.

I'm particularly preoccupied with this topic at the moment, because I am poised over my infant daughter's potty, wondering how to avoid inflicting the same nightmares on her. Now any fool knows that the essential strategy with toddlers is to take up a position and impose your authority with all the ruthlessness of the Inland Revenue. Never ask a toddler if she'd like to do something. She'll only refuse.

But when it comes to this most sensitive of sensitive subjects, I freeze with fatal indecision. 'Would you like to sit on your potty, darling? You don't have to, of course, it doesn't matter. Whatever you like. Sit on it if you like, or not – I mean, you might prefer to leave it till tomorrow. What do you think?'

'NO!' she yells, to be on the safe side, and from the unassailable sanctuary of this Existentialist denial, she relieves herself in her nappy, in perfect privacy. Oh happy creature! It's an ideal system. I can see that, from her point of view, to replace this carefree liberty with our adult anxieties makes no sense at all.

And in my most desperate moments it makes no sense

to me, either. Is the price of civilisation too high? Would I rather be a baboon crouching on a beetling cliff somewhere in Africa? Or would I miss Mozart too much? Ah, Mozart! Now you can bet your life *he* had lavatory dreams. Maybe I should just relax and accept it. After all, as Mozart himself observed: *Cosi Fan Tutte* – Everybody Does It.

Being naughty

Naughty is so much more interesting a concept than *nice*. As a child I could spell *naughty*; but I couldn't for a moment aspire to it. I was saddled with an elder brother who had cornered the market in naughtiness. As a baby he was revoltingly greedy and often gorged till he was sick. He crawled early – and, I'm sure, evilly.

I did it. I confess everything (well . . . *nearly* everything). I was bad. Yes, me! Dear little smock-frocked, white-socked me! I was ten years old at the time. My hair was tied with crisp ribbons on either side of my head – a sure sign of virtue. I came top in Spelling every week. My hair shone, my shoes shone, and the eyes of my teachers shone. If ever there was a goody-goody, I was it. It was driving me right round the bend.

Bad was beautiful: I knew. Literature made that clear. Even in schoolgirl stories, the glamorous character was always the dark, sulking, evil girl called Elvira, who tossed her head and scowled a lot and ended up being expelled.

Life agreed with literature: *naughty* is so much more interesting a concept than *nice*. As a child I could spell *naughty*; but I couldn't for a moment aspire to it. I was saddled with an elder brother who had cornered the market in naughtiness. As a baby he was revoltingly greedy and often gorged till he was sick. He crawled early – and, I'm sure, evilly.

He burnt holes in the carpet with an iron. He didn't write his thank-you letters. He didn't just smoke – he *forced his teddy bear to smoke*. He got bad reports. He went down with appendicitis in the middle of his A levels (how naughty can you get?). And, in the fullness of time, he joined a jazz band. Crumbs! No wonder I was jealous.

How could I compete? I cultivated dirty fingernails. Secretly, I didn't clean my teeth. But nobody noticed. Then I got this idea, in the middle of Mental Arithmetic (at which I was not all that good – but, alas, not nearly bad *enough*). I would forge a love letter to Angela!

23

My bosom friend, Angela, was aptly named, with hair so blond it was a sort of heavenly white. She was quiet, meek, and gentle, with legs so thin you were afraid they would snap when she ran. She was the only person beside whom I felt slightly bad. It was a good feeling. No wonder I liked her. And she deserved a love letter. It would be a laugh.

Dear Angela, I wrote, I love you deeply. Will you please be my girlfriend and marry me? I would like to walk home with you and kiss you goodbye every night. Love from David.

This was, by our standards, Really Rude. I had disguised my handwriting, of course. There were seven Davids in our class, and I was looking forward to intense speculation at break as Angela and I discussed possible candidates, giggling over our milk. It was the work of a moment to slip it into her desk as we went off to Assembly (where *God Be In My Head* was waiting for me).

On our return, Angela found it, glanced at it, and without even showing it to me, took it straight to the teacher, Mr Goodwin. Obliged by the sheer urgency of his name to ensure the triumph of Virtue over Beastliness, Mr Goodwin questioned each of the Davids in turn.

'Come on, David Stevens! Admit it!'

'I didn't, sir! Honest!'

'Oh yes you did, boy! Don't lie to me!'

Mr Goodwin's eyes flashed: clouds covered the sun: the miserable Stevens cowered in the face of magisterial wrath.

'I never sir! 'Snot fair! I never!'

The drawer in the teacher's desk was slowly pulled open, with a portentous rumble in the stillness, and we all sat transfixed as The Slipper rose menacingly into the daylight.

'Admit it, Stevens – or else! We all know what happens to boys who tell lies!'

'But I never done it sir honest I never snot fair I'll tell my dad I never done it no I never.'

Mr Goodwin, bearing The Slipper aloft, advanced slowly down the aisle towards the hapless lad. Transfixed by the Malignancy of the Universe, David Stevens could only cringe. Even his clothes cringed. His blazer, normally a healthy purple, paled to a mere mauve. Above him The Slipper quivered in the stratosphere like one of Jove's thunderbolts about to drop. I sat biting my knuckles in an agony of guilt and fear. So this was being bad. It was dreadful. *Please God let him give up, I prayed silently. Let this inquisition end, even if it has to give way to more Mental Arithmetic.*

If I'd been really bad, of course, I'd have enjoyed every minute. As it was, I was torn between two awful possibilities: of David Stevens being punished unjustly, or of me being found out, and the ingenious and corrupt nature of my crime leading, as it was bound to lead, to expulsion!

My mother was a teacher at the school – she played the piano in assembly. *What would your mother say?* thundered God in my head, so loudly I was sure it must be being broadcast, nay trumpeted, from either ear.

'SMACKKKKK!'

The slipper descended with a deafening report on the edge of David Stevens's desk.

'Stay behind afterwards, Stevens,' said Mr Goodwin. 'We'll soon get to the bottom of this.'

There followed a spelling test of unprecedented ferocity. My hand shook. I could not even spell my name. I was realising with every thump of the heart, the sheer guts and nerve it takes to be bad – and found out. To be stared at! Given The Slipper – on the bum! I nearly fainted at the thought.

As time passed, a dangerously beguiling thought dawned on me: I had got away with it! Nobody knew. I was still shiny Susan, giving off the Odour of Sanctity like clouds of Chanel No 5. What was God up to?

Was He planning to strike me down with boils the moment I fell in love? Or would He wait till I died, and then put me over His marbly knee and wield the heavenly slipper unmercifully with the whole of the Heavenly Host looking on? Or . . . most exciting possibility of all: *hadn't He noticed?*

As I got older, I discovered the much greater choice of naughtinesses available. God has either been very ingenious or terribly careless. As an adult I have succumbed to more attacks of rudeness, silliness and naughtiness which should have exploded harmlessly in the playground years ago. My naughty brother grew up right on cue: becoming sober and decent and only playing jazz now and then. I, entering adulthood from the lofty pinnacle of Ideal Child, had no alternative but to Grow Down. That's my excuse, anyway.

Trying to find peace and quiet

'Can I see your tummy button?' she enquired with pristine clarity. 'And has it got fluff in?'

It was a case of the sound and the fury. Though *sound* is putting it mildly. Cacophony would be more like it. The telephone shrilled as soon as it was put down, like a petulant child. The answering machine answered back. The postman hammered on the door with a tottering pagoda of letters all clamouring for a response. A Dutchman, a French girl and three Americans came to stay. And to crown it all, the European Pneumatic Drill Championships were being held outside our front gate.

The fury was my husband's. He composes avant-garde music, and though some of his pieces do rather resemble a pair of vacuum cleaners locked in mortal combat, that is not what he wants to hear when he performs the fastidious art of tuning in his composer's ear. Nor does he really welcome the song of his infant daughter soaring effortlessly above the domestic racket, glorying in her Gloucestershire accent and rapidly expanding music hall repertoire.

'*Oh Oi Do Loike To Be Besoide The Seasoide,*' she roared outside his door. He burst from his room with a face like thunder and ran to the bottom of the garden. I cornered him by the rhubarb.

'Ijt is impossible!' he cried. (He is Dutch.) 'How kan I kompose in such an environment? Peace I must hav, and quiet. Away we must go, for a weekend, or my head will borst.'

Now, this worried me slightly. He is normally the most orderly and consistent of men, living a life of demure ritual. Even his sleep conforms to a discreet pattern: a peck on my cheek, lights out, silence for four hours, and then a soft intake of breath at an extraordinary dream. Three sips of water from a tumbler by the bed, and then he's back in the arms of Morpheus until 6.48am precisely.

'And what's moer,' he added, 'we are leaving the babje at hoem.'

'What?' I gasped. I knew what we really needed was the wind, the waves, and the unblemished solitude of an autumnal beach, but I couldn't help reflecting that she did loike to be besoide the seasoide herself, dear little pudding.

The issue of what to do was still unresolved when I telephoned The Haven, a guest house near the Devon coast that specialised in wholefoods.

'Do you,' I faltered, rather ambiguously perhaps, 'do you . . . er, have babies?'

'Of course, Medom, sahtainly,' came the answer, just a fraction too late, so that you knew what she really meant was *Crumbs, that's torn it another brat, cor stone the crows*.

'They say they love children,' I lied to my spouse.

'Now my darlijng,' he intoned menacingly to his daughter, 'we are going for a very special holiday, Mama and Dada. You can come too, but only if you are very, very quiet. OK?'

'OK Dada,' she breathed, and broke into a whispered version of *Moi Old Man Said Follow The Van*.

The Haven was surrounded by very still woods. Our room surveyed a grove of bamboos: a positively Buddhist serenity washed over us. I sighed deeply.

'Sssshhh!' admonished my husband.

At suppertime, however, the peace and quiet became almost too deep. All twelve guests sat at one long table, to emphasise our wholeness, and to my surprise most of the others were elderly couples who sat up so straight and said so little, it was like dining with a collection of brass rubbings.

Our infant daughter, seated at the head of the table, sensed a captive audience and the need to fill the silence.

'That man's got skin on his head!' she roared at a bald colonel. Then she leaned winsomely towards an austere lady in lovat green tweeds. We recognised her look, and cringed.

'Can I see your tummy button?' she enquired with pristine clarity. 'And has it got fluff in?'

Receiving no reply, she launched into a vigorous version of *Howd Your Hand Out, You Naughty Boy*.

We wafted her upstairs much in the way that a burning cake is rushed from the kitchen, but the damage was done.

'Ij cannot show my face here any more,' hissed my husband in my ear. 'Ij am kompletely humiliated.'

'Oim Burlington Bertie, Oi Roise at 10.30,' boomed a yokel from the cot. We wedged her teddy bear between her lips and, at length, she slept.

And so did we. The peck on the cheek was delivered as usual, for even in the depths of marital discord he is still a fair man. Lights out: silence for four hours, then the soft intake of breath. Time for the three sips of water.

'Dear me!' he whispered, or words to that effect, 'there is noe water here. Ij will goe to the bathroom.'

Considerately silent, he crept out. And then, all hell broke loose. The shrillest, loudest fire alarm bell I'd ever heard burst out.

'Ij am very sorry – Ij thought it was the light switch,' I heard my husband say.

'What's going on?' bawled an army voice above the din. And it was joined by others.

'Got a screwdriver? ... It must switch off somewhere down by the meters ... Go back to bed, Audrey, it's all a mistake ... Feller set it orf by accident. Foreign chap.' The night was lurid with the clash of walking-frames as elderly guests fled the conflagration.

My heart bled for my better half. He of all people, who apologises whenever he clears his throat, even if he's alone in the room.

Eventually it stopped, and he crept back to bed. We lay in appalled silence as the house settled back into sleep.

'We'll get up at dawn,' I promised, *sotto voce*, 'leave them a blank cheque, and vanish.'

We missed the dawn. We almost missed breakfast. But when we finally descended, we were astonished by the buzz of merry conversation emanating from the dining room. As we entered, a cheer went up – we were welcomed royally. Everyone had their Fire Alarm tale to tell: you could imagine the story going down the dinner parties of decades to come. We were not, after all, in disgrace, but heroes. We had rescued them from all that peace and quiet.

Gardening

At this time of year when, apart from the Christmas rose, only a few dead stalks adorn the earth, horticultural enthusiasm is kept alive by the mouthwatering catalogues which drop through the letter box every day. In fact, browsing through catalogues of old roses in the depth of winter is the most entrancing and intense pleasure gardening can offer.

I am infatuated by gardening, though it wasn't love at first sight. I remember one day when I was a teenager, looking down from my bedroom to where my parents were working in the vegetable garden, and shaking my head in disbelief.

'Why on earth do they do it?' I mused. 'I mean, they could be sitting at their desks like I am now, dreaming about Keith Foster from the Boys' Grammar School, and filling in all the O's on page one of King Lear.'

For several years to come, trees remained only things to meet young men under; flowers, if bought by the young men, a Promising Sign; and a shrubbery – well, I could hardly read the word without blushing. Even prim and proper Jane Austen sends her couples rushing off to the shrubbery to plight their troths. I was hoping that one day someone would offer me his arm and whisper, 'Miss Bennett – 'twas all a misunderstanding – 'tis you I . . . Let us, I beg, adjourn to the Shrubbery.' But as for planting a shrubbery, it scarcely occurred to me that anyone ever had.

But then – I wish I could remember the exact moment – deep in my subconscious, something stirred. At the time my ignorance of horticulture was colossal. I knew a few facts: trees, for example, were always deciduous or carnivorous; flowers were different colours; vegetables could be eaten.

I started off with a flowerpot at my back door with a petunia in it. I watered it, deadheaded it and gazed at it with reckless excitement. I lay awake at night thinking about the petunia. I went off my food. When one day I found a slug on its leaf, so great was my jealous indignation that I threw the slug right over the nearby Co-op.

Soon there were four window boxes, a tub and sixteen flowerpots (I didn't have a garden at the time). They all contained petunias. I took on new responsibilities: a husband and an allotment. It had no shed, and we had no car, so we cycled there with spades, forks, rakes and hoes precariously balanced on our handlebars. We looked like medieval knights at a joust, and returned only slightly less battered after doing battle for hours with the couch grass.

Every gardener is familiar with couch grass. It has to be dug out, every last scrap, or it will reproduce itself in a frenzy of self-confidence. Thank goodness the arrangements for human reproduction are more laborious. I would not like to wake in the morning to find that my finger-nail clippings of yesterday had turned into ten little Sue Limbs all clambering out of the wastepaper basket, wanting their breakfasts. But that's what couch grass is like. Digging it up and burning it proved richly enjoyable. I often think that gardening is a perfect mix of masochism and sadism.

Once I'd realised the momentousness of what had happened to me, my first reaction was dismay that I'd only got one lifetime to cram it into. In the garden, everything takes years and years to learn. Melons, for example. The first year I learned what happens when you don't water them enough: fragrant golf balls. The second year I learned what happens if you water them too much: catastrophic splits and oozes, goo all over the shelving, and the greenhouse swarming with wasps and ants.

In no time at all I had a greenhouse, you see. I was single again by now, but there were always the horticultural consolations. I had bought a house in north London because its back garden was a hundred feet long, hardly noticing whether there was a house attached to it.

My first impulse was to fill it with flowers of all colours, one specimen of each sort, crowded together pell-mell, shrieking pink next to the sort of nauseating orange normally only worn by men mending the road in a fog.

My taste grew refined, however. I started a rigorous colour bar, elevating blues and pinks and banishing oranges and yellows to behind the shed. Nowadays, I allow only the kind of pink that might be found in a faded box of powder left over from the Thirties, and my blue is that usually found on the temples of very old French countesses, where a faint vein glows obscurely through the parchment skin.

I have also discovered leaves. I used to regard them as beside the point, but now they bewitch me. Oft have I gazed upon a hedgerow and exclaimed at the swords and hands and hearts and lace I have seen scattered there. (I refer to the *shape of leaves* – not to the debris left by some aristocratic picnickers caught up in a crime of passion.)

My roses are no longer the pert, pointed, modern Hybrid Teas, with their toughness and watertightness and boring stamina. Give me a Musk or a China or a Provence that opens into a whirl of blush pink and sends out its exquisite scent for a moment, even if within an hour it has crumpled, in the rain, to a handful of sodden tissue paper. Just the names, to a garden snob, are enough. The *Baroness de Rothschild* guards my gate – not a bad class of concierge, really.

But the snobbery reached its zenith with the discovery of the Japanese Garden. Stones, which I had been in the habit of chucking over the fence into my neighbour's garden after dark, were suddenly resonant with meaning.

In a market in Amsterdam, I bought a Buddha's head, carved in volcanic stone. I carried it home in a bag marked *The Body Shop*. I brought a Dutchman home with me from Amsterdam, as well.

Now I am a wife again, and a mother, but my family knows its place. Husband and daughter stare out through the double glazing into the garden, where my frenzied figure is glimpsed occasionally scrabbling amongst the rocks, planting ferns around Buddha. My hair is flattened by the rain, my fingernails are broken, but there is a wild light in my eyes – a sign of the grand passion which has come to rule my life. And my daughter, filling in all the O's on the first page of *The Tale Of Tom Kitten*, wonders what on earth I am up to.

What Christmas is really about

Christmas in Devon was off.

What a dilemma! I ran to the freezer. My first impulse was to immolate myself in its snows, in the grand old tradition of British explorers, leaving a poignant note in the freezer book. *Do not deserve to live. Have no bird – what Xmas is all about.*

It was late on Christmas Eve. The tills were all shut, and in the bank vaults the stacks of notes lay round about, deep and crisp and even. But for us, this year was the year of the great escape. My friend Gloria had invited us down to Devon, whither we would drive at the crack of dawn and stay for several days. This emancipated me from all preparations. Gloria's would be the tinsel, the turkey and the Beaujolais with which we would make merry. All we had to do was pack, and my husband was upstairs doing just that because he is so good at folding things. In all modesty I think I can claim to be better at arranging things.

I was just arranging my feet rather fetchingly on the mantelpiece when the phone rang: Gloria. Her stepfather had had one of his nasty turns, and they would simply have to dash off to Tunbridge Wells for the next few days. Sorry, but Christmas in Devon was off. *Sic transit Gloria* . . .

What a dilemma! I ran to the freezer. My first impulse was to immolate myself in its snows, in the grand old tradition of British explorers, leaving a poignant note in the freezer book. *Do not deserve to live. Have no bird – what Xmas is all about.* Then – and what one wants at a time like this is a miracle – I *saw* one. Right in the far corner, its wings, as it were, waving at me from a drift of frosted beans and corn. I whipped it out and discovered that it was a chicken. All right, it wasn't a turkey. But what's so special about a turkey, apart from the bits of red rubber hanging down its face?

There was just one problem. It was deep frozen. And I knew as well as the next housewife that poultry has to be thoroughly defrosted for days, nay weeks. The thought of my family turning blue from salmonella poisoning, dropping to their knees and gurgling inarticulately during the Queen's speech was too awful to contemplate – though, come to think of it, that's probably how they'd behave if Her Majesty ever crossed our threshold for real – which I hope she *won't* – not without ringing first, anyway. I can't stand droppers-in.

The chicken slipped from my numbed fingers and hit the kitchen floor with an almighty crack. It was at this point that the doorbell rang. A dropper-in! My snarl rising dangerously close to my collar, I ran to the door. I could hear singing outside. This lot had evidently brought some high-tech torches with them, because as I opened the door I was almost blinded by the glare.

'Fear not,' I heard a voice begin, but I cut him short. I wasn't having any of that born-again stuff here, thank you very much. It was bad enough being born the first time.

'Sorry!' I cried firmly. 'I gave you something yesterday!' And I slammed the door in their faces.

Well, I'd done my bit for carol singers already, including two small punky boys with savage countenances who had chanted 'We will rock you rock you rock you!' with such practised menace, I was afraid that unless I gave them at least 50p, there was a danger of my being rocked there and then on my very own doorstep.

Back to the bird. I prepared a sort of bath of cold water for it in the kitchen sink (something one should never do) and hastily turned my thoughts to the problem of drink.

Drink *is* a problem, don't you find, if you haven't done your Christmas shopping and you discover that there's only a bottle of Frascati in the cupboard? Getting legless is, after all, what Christmas is all about.

At least there was mineral water: I put the bottles in the fridge. I'll say this for mineral water: it does restore the *frisson* of living dangerously. Some brands are so explosive, they should be given only to disgraced gentlemen who face trial for high treason. 'Guy knew what he had to do. It was all over. They left him alone in his room with a bottle of cold mineral water. He muttered a Latin tag, raised the bottle to his lips . . . and blew his brains out.'

With the bird thawing and the water chilling, I could turn my attention to decorations, which luckily could stay at room temperature. I was Sellotaping them to the ceiling, standing on the table in a crouching attitude made necessary by the fact that the ceiling is rather too low when viewed from the top of the table. And then, the doorbell rang. *Again.*

It made me jump so much, I nearly butted my way through the plaster and obtained an unexpected insight into the room above, where my infant daughter lay asleep. At least I hoped she was asleep, and dreaming of fat old men in white beards bringing knickknacks for her greedy little fingers to pull apart by lunch time – for that's what Christmas is all about, isn't it?

I was still rubbing my head and cursing when I opened the front door. And then my heart sank. Well, you get used to hippies living in the West Country, but you don't expect them to turn up on your own doorstep, I mean, not on Christmas Eve. By the look of them they'd been on the road for some months, and I don't think they'd have recognised a bathroom if they'd seen one. There were two of them – worse than one – but better than five hundred, I suppose.

One was a girl, and judging by the shape of her, she'd be in the labour ward before the night was over. The chap with her was much older, and I don't expect they were married. I bet it wasn't even his, but that sort don't seem to care about Victorian family values. Otherwise they'd be tucked up in a nice little flat somewhere Sellotaping balloons to the ceiling and doing all those other things that Christmas is all about.

I didn't give them a chance to open their mouths. I grabbed my head and muttered, 'Sorry – migraine – can't help – people next door very nice – maternity hospital first on the left.' And I dived back indoors to check on the bird.

Speaking of birds, a strange thing happened a couple of hours later. I heard a sort of singing in the sky – I expect it was our local carol bus, it's got a sound system that could fill the Albert Hall – and then two feathers fell down the chimney. And you know, they sort of *glowed*, like phosphorus, in the dark.

It wasn't until my child peeped out of her bedroom a little while later and whispered in a voice feverish with longing, 'Has Jesus come down the chimney yet?' that I remembered, after all, what Christmas was really all about.

The language barrier and getting on with in-laws

Would his dad shake his head over my vegetable patch? Would his mama quail at our near-vertical hillside? Would I be able to deal with the food problems? I'd been warned that they could not deal with pips, and pride myself that I am one of the few daughters-in-law who has ever set out to pluck, draw and truss a pound of frozen raspberries.

Visits from the in-laws are always a little dicey, aren't they? You know that they think you're not really good enough for His Nibs, especially in the plum-bottling and dustbin-scrubbing department. My in-laws are even more disconcerting than most, since they speak only Dutch. For seventy years they had never ventured beyond their quiet little stretch of north Holland, but now they were coming to darkest Gloucestershire, for a whole week's holiday.

My husband had gone to fetch them from the airport. I had stayed behind to finish off those last little bits of nail-biting. Would his dad shake his head over my vegetable patch? Would his mama quail at our near-vertical hillside? Would I be able to deal with the food problems? I'd been warned that they could not deal with pips, and pride myself that I am one of the few daughters-in-law who has ever set out to pluck, draw and truss a pound of frozen raspberries.

At least they will enjoy the pure air, I thought, flinging their bedroom window open wide – and then quickly banging it shut as I reeled back from the powerful smell of dung from the neighbouring field. Would it hang about, or could I disperse it with a few dexterous swishes of folded newspaper? I swished and sniffed, but all I could smell now was the polish I'd zealously applied to the bedside table. (I may not bottle plums, but by gum I can polish a table.) Might all this polish overpower them in their sleep? Might they – O Heaven – expire in a cloud of English Lavender?

'Mum!' I cried. 'Do vacuum cleaners actually suck up *smells*?'

My parents share our house, so I often appeal to my

mother on questions of domesticity – not that she's that keen on it, preferring to read French novels. But what use was French now? Dutch was double Dutch to her. To my dad likewise. And to me. In three years of marriage I had learned only enough Dutch to make myself misunderstood wherever I went. Very soon after the in-laws arrived, I whispered urgently to my spouse:

'Don't leave me alone with them! Delightful though they are, when you go out of the room, I feel stranded! You must be around to translate, or I'm lost!' I even resented my husband's trips to the bathroom. 'You're going to have a bath, darling? What a good idea! Why don't we all come along? They do in California!'

But later, after an almost silent lunch during which I kept hearing myself say in Dutchlish, '*Sori vor de smell ov dong*,' the scenario I had dreaded began to unfold.

Everyone was having a kip – except me and the two grandmas. My ma-in-law smiled across the sitting room at my mother.

'*Ik heb enn cadeautje voor U gekocht*,' she said, waving a bar of chocolate. (I have since learned that this means 'I've bought a little present for you.')

'Mum – take it!' I hissed.

'Are you sure?' said Mum. I wasn't actually. I wasn't even sure it was chocolate. Foreign food is so different, this might turn out to be a slim volume of Dutch poetry.

My mother took the chocolate and smiled graciously back.

'*Houdet U van zoetigheid?*' enquired my ma-in-law. (Apparently, 'Have you got a sweet tooth?')

'She asked me something then!' said my mother in a panic.

The last bit sounded like central heating. I went Dutchlish again. '*We hebben zentral heiding, ja, bekos de winters aar zo kold*,' I faltered.

My mother-in-law giggled unnvervingly. Had I accidentally said something faintly obscene? A silence fell. This was more like it. A companionable silence is so infinitely preferable to talk. But she was off again.

' '*t is toch ongelooflijk hoe de melkboer 't voor mekaar krijgt al die heuvels op te rijden*.' (This, I later discovered, was 'Extraordinary how the milkman manages to drive up all these hills.')

'Crumbs, that was a big 'un!' I whispered, but I had picked up a familiar word: *heuvels*. It means hills.

My ma-in-law was smiling in anticipation of more delightful gobbledegook. I wanted to say the hills were beautiful, but the only Dutch adjective I could remember was the word for tired. It's a word I seem to use quite a lot. I forget how to spell it, but it sounds like moo. Now, I obviously couldn't say the hills were tired. But I am nothing if not resourceful. I would say they were *tiring*.

'*De hills*,' I spluttered, '*aar* . . . *mooing*.'

Time passed.

'Did you know she's got sixteen grandchildren?' I asked my mother in desperation. Then I turned to my ma-in-law.

'*U heb sixteen grandchildren, nicht war?*'

I waved sixteen fingers at her – not all at once, of course.

'*Ja, Ja*,' she beamed. '*Carla, Laura, Yvonne, Arnold, Mirjam, Cyrille, Phillipe, Jos, Sabine, Petra, Coen, Josette, Wendy, Astrid, Bavonia en Betsy.*'

'It must be rather expensive at Christmas,' remarked my mother drily, outbred but not outboxed. We had, however, stumbled on a magic formula: names.

'Queen Juliana! Princess Beatrix!' (My mother's knowledge of the Dutch royal family is not quite up to date.)

'*Ja, ja!* Elizabeth! Fergie! Winston Churchill!'

'Vermeer! Van Gogh!'

'*Ja!* Glen Hoddle!'

It was a disappointment that she had not heard of Steve Davis. But the bridges were well and truly built.

At this moment my husband surfaced. His mother greeted him without any urgency and prattled away happily.

'My mother says you had a very nice talk,' he beamed, scraping me off the hearth rug. 'She is very impressed with your Dutch.' He beamed. I beamed. We all beamed.

As for the rest of the week, the sun shone, the food processor whizzed successfully and the smell of dung faded to a faint rural whiff, what Keats might have called one of the Pongs of Spring.

It's a great thing, the language barrier. It ends all possibility of that worst hazard of a visit from the in-laws: those little misunderstandings.

Word processors

For a long time I thought Word Processors were a bit like Food Processors: you fed a long word such as ANTHROPO-LOGICAL down the tube, whizzed the steel blade for a couple of minutes, then shook out ANT, LOG, HOP, POLO, LOGO, AN, TO, GO and PATH into a clean bowl. A wonderful aid for crossword freaks, but I've never mastered crosswords. They don't just make me cross, they reduce me to a foam-flecked fury. Indeed, words are treacherous things, and every writer needs all the help he or she can get to round the damn things up and keep them in their places.

But it wasn't until I started to write for *Good House-keeping* that I finally capitulated to the idea of a word processor. In the past I'd been in the habit of writing my work on an ancient typewriter, with lovably furry keys and a habit of going PING at the end of every line and jumping right off the table. This was a bit too grimy and primitive for the rather dazzling ladies at *GH*. So I took the plunge, patted my venerable old typewriter goodbye, and went and bought a word processor.

The trouble was, we couldn't get it in the boot of the car – not in its box, anyway. So we had to unpack it, in the rain, in the rush hour, and then tuck it in cosily with a tartan rug around its keys and drive it home at twenty-five mph as if it was the most precious grandma in the world. In fact in some ways it does resemble a grandma. It seems to need very little sleep and, though it sits winking in the corner in a very modest way, it can keep children amused for hours. It has a formidable memory and can have the most appalling acts of stubbornness.

Its architecture, however, is decidedly non-gran. It upset me quite a lot at first to see its remorselessly grey modern angles invading my acres of worm-eaten pine. It was uncompromisingly 1980s and functional and, until I plucked up my courage and tried to use it, its presence in the house was bound to seem enigmatic. It had come with a manual which offered the baffled beginner a lifeline. I picked it up – and almost broke my back.

The manual was over six hundred pages long! Six hundred pages, without any cheeky dialogue, rich bitches, corpses in swimming pools, or bonking. How could I possibly manage to read it?

I peeped timidly into it, opening the pages at random. 'Chapter Five:' it said, 'The CP/M Plus built-in commands and utilities.' Crumbs. I didn't like the sound of that. Was it going to order me about then? Would messages bark at me from the screen? HAVE YOU CLEANED THE KITCHEN FLOOR TODAY? NO? WELL JOLLY WELL GET ON WITH IT . . . I flipped a few pages further on.

My husband, who was leaning over my shoulder and breathing more heavily than since the first halcyon days of our marriage (he is excited by technology), pointed out that before we did anything with the word processor we had to feed it a disc – the Start of the Day disc. A bit like breakfast. I slid the disc into the slot. Oh yes, I was getting the hang of this. The machine got stuck right in. GOBBLE GOBBLE GOBBLE GOBBLE, it went. BUUUURP. BURP BURP BUUUUURP.

Gradually, I began to tiptoe over the keyboard. Tipfinger, I mean, of course. What I wrote appeared on the screen! And when I made a typing mistake, lo! one tap of the DELEYTE, sorry, DELETE key and it was wiped off. No more grisly little white bottles of correction fluid. And when I made the giant leap from typing to printing, and the printer chattered away all by itself, leaving me free to pick my fingers and stare out of the window, my gratitude knew no bounds. 'Oh, thank you, darling!' I cried. 'You are wonderful!'

The honeymoon period was soon over, though. My word processor offered me a lot of sophisticated services. Why, in the first half of the manual alone there were five appendices. I was in danger of developing acute appendicitis. And getting the machine to do simple things as number the pages was the devil's own job. You see, I have to admit it: I didn't go through the manual step by step. I skipped the boring bits and stuck to the sex and violence, like I always do. As a result, I often approached the word processor with only a vague intuitive feel of how to get things done. At such times it would BEEP rudely at me. Irate little messages would flash up on the screen. FIND PAGE???? it would say, its eyebrows arched in disdain. SHOW BLOCKS, it would demand. Now I'm not in the habit of showing my blocks to just anybody. Not unless they show me theirs, first.

Sometimes it would just refuse to print. It would sulk. PRINTER IDLE, it would inform me airily.

'There's no need to flaming well boast about it!' I would screech, tearing my hair as the wasted hours unfolded. 'I hate you! You're just plain pig-stupid sometimes!'

The worst of it was, I knew it was really my fault that the printer wasn't working. I had neglected some vital detail of my instructions and, without it, the machine just sat there with its arms folded and a tiresome pout on its lips. I can't stand people like that.

'Why can't you give a little?' I'd yell. 'Make allowances for human error once in a while? But oh, no – all I have to do is put one foot wrong and you never let me forget it!' At this point, I'm sure, the neighbours were going to slip a note under the door with the number of the Marriage Guidance Council . . .

The word processor is at its worst when checking my spelling. Never is the gulf which divides us more apparent. I have come to realise that I am, linguistically speaking, a kind of compost heap of 'je ne sais quoi's, cripeses and gorblimeys. These words it does not like. Gorblimey, it suggests, should be replaced with gobies. (What are gobies? At least everyone knows what gorblimeys are – kind of poor men's Hail Marys.) But names are its downfall. I made a reference recently to the French Impressionist painter Monet. Monet? said the word processor, don't you mean money? Typical, I reckon, of its value system.

Any names, not just French ones, alarm it. Margaret Thatcher would, if it had its way, be Macerate Thatcher; Norman Tebbit would be Normal Teabag – not a name, I feel, which does full justice to the gentleman concerned. And yet there is something about its heavy-handed, awkward attempts to help, even when way out of its depth, that finally endears it to me. If ever I get lost in its mazes of DATA FILES and UNIT MARKERS, I throw Stanislavsky or Shostakovitch at it. Stainlessly? Shortcoming? it whimpers pathetically. Then I put Shortcoming's Cello Concerto on the record player and let it wash gloriously over me, secure in the knowledge that I am, after all, the boss.

Getting away from it all

I don't think eggs can be eaten without salt. It is the philosopher's stone which turneth eggs to gold. Without it they are mere elemental slime.

The whole idea of the self-catering holiday cottage is that it's supposed to be a home from home, isn't it? It certainly offers privacy, which even the best guesthouses cannot provide: you can lie face down on the hearthrug and swear horribly, just as if you were at home. But try and do that in Mrs Higgins's spruce little B & B establishment, and she may call the ambulance.

So for our spring break I decided that, much as I loved the Mrs Higginses of this world, I wanted to be *chez moi* and yet, somehow, utterly away from it all.

The self-catering cottage in question was in the Highlands. It lay four miles off the B road, up and up a rough track. We could only travel at about four mph, owing to the ruts, the boulders, the decomposing eagles, and the fact that our car is so very saloon, it's practically a lounge lizard. What we obviously needed, as our axles groaned above yet another boulder, was a Chieftain tank. Still, eventually the romantic outline of Macweirdie Farm rose before us. It crouched quaintly under a blasted thorn. Well, that's the whole point of self-catering, isn't it? Away from it all, if you want BATH-ROOM ENSUITE WITH VIEW OF PROMENADE, then you'll end up in Eastbourne, won't you?

'Water!' snapped my thirsty child. I raced for the door, and after the statutory ten minutes wrestling with the alien keys, we burst in and turned on a tap. An empty chugging sound shook the house. The water evidently had to be turned on at the mains. But where? We searched fruitlessly through gloomy cupboards and under stinking stairs. But no tap appeared. We did, however, find a grimy sheaf of papers which held not only the secrets of domestic life at Macweirdie Farm, but also a table of Thou Shalt Nots which put the Old Testament God firmly in His place as a permissive old softie.

'The water,' read my husband with difficulty in the waning light, 'can be turned on as follows: leave the farm by the north gate and go across the first field (beware of ram). Climb the five-bar gate into the next field. Approximately seven yards to the east of the gate you will see a large stone. Under this stone is a manhole cover. Lift this off and you will be able to reach down inside and turn the water on.'

He set forth into the twilight apprehensively. At last there was a sigh, a splutter and a great shaking, and the taps gushed generously. It was brown for ten minutes, adding to the sense of wild remoteness.

Indeed there was much natural majesty around. The air was full of buzzards and bustards, and it was a short stumble from the front doorstep to any number of reeling precipices. But it was a hell of a long drive to the nearest shop and my notions of necessities were urgently revised after a brief glance into the food cupboard to see what it might offer for supper.

A home from home should have everything in the cupboard that you have at home, shouldn't it? Macweirdie Farm certainly didn't. Salt was the thing I missed most, since the only protein not actually wheeling about in the air reposed in the egg box. I don't think eggs can be eaten without salt. It is the philosopher's stone which turneth eggs to gold. Without it they are mere elemental slime.

And speaking of elemental slime, the kitchen had not been used all winter, and the frost had silted up the burners. It had also shrunk the work surfaces. You cannot pluck a bustard on two square feet of Formica-covered cupboard top. So beans it had to be. And did one wish to think about beans, upon the majestic mountain peaks? One did not.

My husband took to the rock-strewn Scottish wilderness with sheer joy. My own joy was less sheer: about thirty denier at best. The days were wracked with anxiety. Was the fridge really working? Sometimes it seemed the warmest place in the house. How near was the nearest doctor? Come to think of it, my throat was just beginning that demented tingle which heralds a mighty head cold. How near was the nearest lemon? Edinburgh, say?

The picturesque isolation was at its worst at night. We had no TV to fill the solitude and my three thousand unread books were all at home, too. In one of those moments of mental derangement, I had left my holiday reading behind.

So I was bookless. All the cottage yielded was a mildewed copy of *Soft Fruit Growing* by Raymond Bush. I installed myself in a chair and prepared for my initiation into the mysteries of the big bud mite. But the chairs were wrong. They tilted back at such an odd angle my neck began to feel unequal to the task of holding my head on. I moved to the ancient sofa, but so weak were its springs that my bottom plummeted right through to the floor. I wasn't sure that this was getting away from it all.

Suddenly, lying there, I was filled with a poetic longing for a dear little guesthouse, down at the foot of the mountain, maybe. On a nice cosy road somewhere. We would awaken not to the cawing birds of prey, but to the delectable scent of someone else frying our breakfast bacon. A motherly body. Mrs Higgins? Yes . . .

Bring me thy nylon sheets, O Mrs Higgins – burden me with thy breakfasts. I will queue for the loo till kingdom come and not complain. Indeed, for the privilege of membership of your cosy little household I will gladly pay through the ear, nose and throat. Oh, and just one other thing – have you got some Beechams Powders? You have? And a hot water bottle, too? O thank you, Mrs H – you're an absolute angel.

Being terrified of Aunt Ursula

Now, as a girl, I'd wasted
hours on Ancient Greek,
when I should've been
learning laundry science.
So, in the wool shop, I had
only gazed in
admiration at the Aegean
blue of the yarn and not
noticed that it was Real
Wool – the sort that can only
safely be washed in a
mountain stream by a
barefoot maiden.

Who's afraid of Virginia Woolf? Well, actually, I'm sure I would've been. Tall women in large hats terrify me. Take my Aunt Ursula, my mother's elder sister. She lives a mere half-hour away, and every first Sunday in the month she rolls up at our door: regular as clockwork and just as well equipped for a ticking off. With her, disapproval isn't just a way of life – it's a sacred calling.

On her visits, Aunt Ursula can disapprove of me *and* my mother at one fell swoop, since we share not only a house but a disgracefully cavalier attitude to housework. Aunt Ursula proudly claims she can see herself in her saucepans – rather a terrifying thought, I find.

At home Aunt Ursula performs the work of a whole team. She bakes, bottles, freezes, and brews: she knits, crochets and hems. There is never a moment when some muscle is not twitching with domestic duty. She had a large family, but suffered no nonsense from them. Her children were always folded in rows, like the ironing, and iron was the discipline that enfolded them from their first moments until they left school and slipped away into various building societies.

Her worst disdain is reserved for my maternal failings. My daughter has never grown fast enough for Aunt Ursula. All her babies looked like Sumo wrestlers.

'Poor little mite,' she commiserated earlier this year with my child, who was shivering – understandably with Aunt Ursula looming over her. 'Not enough flesh on her to keep her warm. What she needs is a nice hand-knitted cardie.'

'I'm no good at knitting,' I blushed.

'I'll knit you one,' offered Aunt Ursula. 'I never have anything to do after nine-thirty anyway. I've always vacuumed the house, got lunch ready and done the budgie by nine.'

'Goodness!' I said. 'That would be kind of you, Auntie.'

'You buy the wool and pattern, though, dear,' she insisted. 'I'm sure I'd get the colour wrong. The colours they dress babies in nowadays!'

I dashed off obediently to the wool shop, where I found a rather delightful wool in a striking shade.

'There you are, you see,' sighed Aunt Ursula when she saw it. 'What colour do they call *that?*'

'Kingfisher blue, Auntie,' quoth I, quaking before her colour bar. She shook her head, as if to imply that to wear such a colour was, even for a kingfisher, a sign of irredeemable vulgarity. But she went away and knitted the cardigan.

It was jolly nice, actually, and the babe looked a whiz in it right up to lunchtime. But by 2pm she had more scrambled egg on her shoulders than an admiral of the fleet. In a trice it was in the washing machine, turned up nice and HOT.

Now, as a girl, I'd wasted hours on Ancient Greek, when I should've been learning laundry science. So, in the wool shop, I had only gazed in admiration at the Aegean blue of the yarn and not noticed that it was Real Wool – the sort that can only safely be washed in a mountain stream by a barefoot maiden. Aunt Ursula, understanding wool, washing machines and babies, would've opted for sensible, machine-washable, sugar-pink acrylic.

I fished the unfortunate garment out of the gleaming drum, and my heart gave a lurch of horror. Nobody was ever going to wear it again – except perhaps a gerbil.

My only hope was my mother. Was she prepared to knit an identical substitute . . . in short, was she prepared to pull the wool over Aunt Ursula's eyes? She was. We had a month, after all, before Aunt Ursula's next visit.

But the Fates were against us. The kingfisher-blue wool had been discontinued. 'There must be kingfisher blue somewhere!' I shrieked. 'I'm going to London! Maybe even New York! Maybe even New Zealand!' In a remote corner of New Oxford Street, I found my wool. Just enough and no more.

Back home my mother sharpened her needles and cast on.

'Knit tight, Mum – knit tight!' I urged, 'it must be Ursuline.' (My aunt could've knitted the Berlin wall.)

My mother knitted like a thing possessed, and soon it was finished. I cut the buttons off the original to sew them onto the replacement, and then –

'Good heavens!' cried my Mama. 'Look! Ursula put the buttons down the wrong side!'

Yes. There they were: five little buttonholes all down the left side. Aunt Ursula's cardigan had buttoned *left over right*, of all things – the traditional male way.

'She must've known,' I panicked. '*Known* that I was going to shrink it, and she deliberately set this trap for us, so she'd know this cardigan was a forgery!'

The buttons were sewn on, the cardigan complete – but the wrong way round. Would Aunt Ursula notice this aberration? I considered taking photographs of the cardigan and only ever showing her those . . . I considered always approaching Aunt Ursula via a mirror, as if she was some kind of Medusa . . . I knew she would be fooled by none of this, however.

'It's no use,' I sighed. 'I'm done for.'

But at this moment Aunt Ursula left for her annual holiday – known to the cognoscenti as the Harrowing of Harrogate.

And by the time she returned to the steamy sin-infested south, I was offering thanks to the Fates and Furies, for, miracle of miracles! – the child had grown out of the damned thing! I passed Aunt Ursula a cup of tea, with shaking hand. 'I'm afraid she's outgrown the dear little cardigan, Auntie,' I stammered. 'I gave it to my friend Mary in Swindon.'

'Swindon,' sighed Aunt Ursula, 'Ah well . . .' And she leant over and gave me a very penetrating look. 'If you'd like me to knit you another, dear, you only have to say.'

Keeping the zing in marriage

I slipped into an old pair
of high heels from my Footlights days, and in these and
my Thermolactyl vest I
teetered out, my sexiest
anorak flapping alluringly
in the wind. There was the
hapless Dutchman, bent
over his chain saw.
'*Goedverdommer!*' he cried.
'What has got into you?'

Like most wives, I am haunted occasionally by a question: is my marriage quite all it should be? Not that my spouse isn't utterly charming, and like most Dutchmen, he is very well trained in domestic matters, and properly endowed with a sense of his own mere equality. Not so much my Better Half as my Just-As-Good Half. But the strings of my heart had not gone ZING for as long as I could remember. In fact, the only thing that went ZING in our house was the food processor when my husband was whipping up one of his delectable little soufflés.

Melissa Sadoff came to my aid. She has written a book called *Woman As Chameleon* which addresses itself to this problem. Marriage is not a partnership of equals, Melissa seemed to say. *You should love and obey your husband — indeed worship him*, she insists. *The husband should not be burdened with household chores, or gardening. He should do what pleases him* . . . What? No more soufflés? I had to hide this book. And yet . . . should I follow Melissa's advice and subject my Dutchman to the Sadoff treatment? You never know, I pondered, it might bring back the ZING.

Melissa advises that to deter a husband from straying, a wife should try to behave like a different woman every day. The unsuspecting spouse would be assailed on Wednesdays by an alluring seductress, on Fridays by a childlike playmate, and on Sundays by an intellectual companion. This was going to be difficult. But Melissa provided detailed instructions.

Each morning, I should *get him off to a wonderful start, chattering and frolicking with him, helping him run his bath* . . . OK. It was 7am. My husband stirred in his sleep. I leapt into action. 'Hello, hello, who's your lady friend?' I trilled, switching on the radio and doing a few high kicks. (*The wife should also put on music and dance for her husband*, says Melissa.) Mine opened one eye, and stared in disbelief. I fell on my knees for a spot of veneration.

'Darling!' I whispered, paraphrasing Melissa as closely as memory permitted, 'thank you for providing a comfortable life, especially the car. I love you and am proud to be your wife. Turn over and I will give you a soothing back massage with hand lotion and then breathe hot sensuous breath up and down your spine.' But he was out of the door and into the bathroom like a shot. I followed. 'Let me help you run your bath, beloved!' I frolicked. 'I can turn taps perfectly well myself!' he snapped. 'And the baby is crying. Go and see to her. It is your turn today.' Ah yes. Children. As Melissa points out, *Women can never be too creative when they have children around.* In Melissa's universe, one's offspring come a very poor second to His Nibs.

Indeed, *Men are close to an ideal.* Whereas women, with a few exceptions, *have a tendency to become small-minded, unfaithful and demanding.* And women searching for second husbands (he's my second) *can resemble female vultures or screaming hyenas* . . . I tucked my tail between my legs, rolled my yellow eyes and padded down to the kitchen.

Here, according to Melissa's instructions, I arranged his place setting *as sweetly and attractively as possible,* putting *a note saying 'I love you'* next to a tiny flower in a bud vase. Then I set about making my Emperor breakfast. By the time he came down, though, our toddler had ripped the note up and upset the bud vase all over the place setting.

It was Sunday, so I was all set to be the intellectual companion, although, of course, *the total or real woman will never try to win an argument with her husband.* 'Do you think there is conclusive evidence of a higher organising intelligence in the universe, darling?' I enquired meekly. 'Or are you of the Darwinian persuasion?' He muttered something about mending the chain saw and retired to the garage.

But Melissa is equal to every situation. *If your husband is in the garage,* she suggests, *undress, put on a sexy slip, wrap yourself in your fur coat, slip on suspenders, black stockings and high-heeled shoes and surprise him.*

There are no fur coats in our house, and I was desolate to discover that, with years of disuse, my suspender belts had all perished. My slip had slipped and my tights were loose, but there was an old pair of high heels from my Footlights days, and in these and my Thermolactyl vest I teetered out, my sexiest anorak flapping alluringly in the wind. There was the hapless Dutchman, bent over his chain saw. 'Goedverdommer!' he cried. 'What has got into you?'

'I have come simply to seduce you,' I intoned, in my most sultry and loving voice. By now I spoke fluent Sadoffskian. A woman should always kiss her husband's body starting from his toes. I went for his trainers, but he dodged, jumped into the car and roared off down the drive.

I had blown it. A couple of hours of Woman As Chameleon, and my spouse had disappeared in a puff of carbon monoxide. I had a few scores to settle with Melissa. I stared at her picture on the dust jacket. She looked opulent and well upholstered in a low-cut Transylvanian blouse. I decided character assassination was my best hope of revenge. I snarled gently under my breath, and sharpened my pen.

In the end, I did not have to indulge in any unpleasantness. When my husband returned, I greeted him with a grunt and let him do the washing-up while I lounged about in muddy boots and an old tracksuit, reading Exchange And Mart. Soon we were back to normal, but he's made me promise never to put him on a pedestal again – it gives him vertigo.

'The sad thing,' he mused, gazing a little too wistfully at Melissa's Transylvanian cleavage, 'is that she means well.' But it seemed to me that the really sad thing was that Melissa's book had once been a perfectly good tree.

Being burgled

At the time, I was doing a bit of prison teaching. I had spent the morning coaxing my cons towards literacy, and wishing there were more primary readers designed for this rather specialist use (*Janet And John Put The Frighteners On*).

It was early summer when it happened. It always sends a shiver down my spine to remember it, even now. Brrr! There it goes, like a demented zip fastener. And that's exactly how I felt when I arrived home from work on that fatal day to discover that somebody'd broken in. I lived alone at the time, in London: an ordinary terraced house in a busy street. Somehow, though I knew all the statistics about burglary, I never thought it would happen to me. Or at least, I'd assumed if it happened it would be at night.

I was prepared, mentally, for that. There was a huge bolt on my bedroom door, a phone in the room, and a large chamber pot to contribute to my comfort in the event of a siege, or to crack across the skull of any miscreant who managed to slither through the gaps in the floorboards. It was simple: I'd wake in the night, hear noises, grab the phone, and leap aboard my chamber pot safe in the knowledge that the only things I cared about losing – a few trinkets of great sentimental value – were right there in the room with me, in an old spice chest. In the drawer marked ALOES.

But it didn't turn out like that. At the time, I was doing a bit of prison teaching. This was back in the years Before *Good Housekeeping* – a benighted era I refer to as BGH, and which often felt, financially, a little like GBH. I had spent the morning coaxing my cons towards literacy, and wishing there were more primary readers designed for this rather specialist use (*Janet And John Put The Frighteners On*). It had been an ordinary sort of day, until I arrived home and noticed that my front door was slightly ajar. My heart began to pound. I was used to ex-burglars at work, but here-and-now burglars at home were a completely different matter.

Closer inspection revealed that the lock was hanging off slightly more than I'd have liked, and that the door, which I had only recently painted a cheerful canary yellow, had yielded to the pressure of a mightier limb, and was looking decidedly splintery and apologetic. My first thought, however, was were they still there? Yes, a coward soul is mine. It would be so embarrassing, wouldn't it, to come face to face with your actual burglar? A friend of mine did just that once: walked into her kitchen to find a man crouched on top of the washing machine by the window. 'What are you doing?' she enquired, a fair enough question in the circumstances. 'I'm a burglar!' he grinned rather gauchely, then dived out through the window. I don't think they like it either: social chitchat is a bit of a burden. So I fervently hoped they'd made a clean getaway.

Just in case they hadn't, I strolled loudly into the hall, singing *I'm forever blowing bubbles*, and leaving the front door wide open. 'I think I'll leave the front door wide open!' I mused aloud. 'To let some fresh air in. Maybe I'll even go out in the garden – it's such a lovely day.' Then I ran through the house leaving as many doors and windows open as possible and hid in the garden shed.

After ten minutes I decided that they must have had time to escape. I tiptoed back indoors. The first thing I saw was a rubber glove on the stairs. Had they felt a pang of conscience and done the washing-up before they left? No, of course not. The pagodas of dirty plates in my sink would deter even those on community service programmes. But I didn't touch the rubber glove. I knew all about fingerprints.

I rang the police. Eventually a rather tired-looking chap in a sad raincoat arrived. I accompanied him into my sitting room. He shook his head at the sight: clothes everywhere, drawers pulled out, potted plants knocked over, compost scattered over all the loose papers spilling out of my files.

'Made a bit of a mess, didn't they?' he observed. I didn't dare tell him that the room had looked exactly like that when I'd left for work. 'What did they take, then?' he asked. Now, if you live alone in chaos and aren't sure what you possess, let alone where it is, it's difficult to work out what's missing. But my most important loss was obvious.

'They took a drawer marked ALOES,' I sighed. 'With all my little knick-knacks in it.'

'Any idea of the value of the items?'

'Impossible to say,' I shrugged. 'I mean, there was an old silver locket containing a lock of Captain Oates's hair. How do you value that?'

'Whose?'

'Captain Oates,' I said. 'You know, the chap who said, "I am just going outside, and may be some time," and walked out into the snow. In Antarctica. With Captain Scott.'

'And you had a lock of his hair?'

'His baby hair. I met his sister when I was a schoolgirl. She gave the hair to me.'

'Well, love,' he concluded, 'I'm afraid that lock of hair is on a rubbish tip somewhere. They'd keep the locket, but chuck away what was in it.' And off he went: a slight figure, bowed under the weight of metropolitan crime.

I didn't miss my video. But my knick-knacks, and above all the lock of hair, I mourn to this day.

This experience should have taught me not to value material objects. It was knowing the story of Captain Oates that was magical, not the lock of hair. And they couldn't steal the knowledge. But I have learnt to keep my holy relics in old shoe boxes, not silver lockets. So if any burglars are reading this, as a change from *Good Housebreaking*, there are a few bits of silver on the sideboard – do help yourself.

But please, oh please leave that old shoe box under the bed. It contains my daughter's first thin fair hair, and a sugar frog given to me in 1978 by a special person, which has now changed to the texture of rather unpleasant soapy stone. The really priceless things, in other words.

Learning to Drive

'Thou Hast Failed,' intoned
the Examiner. I was cast
back into Limbo, with the
red L firmly plastered to my
rear, for another three
millennia.

I've done it! At last! I'm a real grown-up now. It wasn't the living alone bit, the divorcing and remarrying bit, the having a baby bit or the making a cake for the first time bit (though nearly). It was the Passing The Driving Test bit. That really does sort out the sheep from the goats.

It wasn't easy. Oh no. They say you need an hour's professional tuition for every year of your life. On that basis I'm just about due for my telegram from the Queen. And what they don't tell you is that, if you also go out with your husband to practise in between lessons, you need an extra two hours' tuition for every hour spent with your spouse – multiplied by the number of years you've been married, and taking away the husband you first thought of.

I had tried to learn when I was an undergraduate, but I gave up after a close shave with a juggernaut in a country lane. Twenty years passed. A whole dynasty of bicycles rolled through my life. I walked, I waited for buses and British Rail. And then came the acts of madness that threw my life totally out of kilter: I married a composer, had a baby and moved to the country.

This time I had to do it. Life was impossible otherwise. When shopping I assume a languid amble. But my husband isn't a 'languid amble' man. He's an 'I must get back to my symphony when Mozart was my age he'd been dead for eight years' sort of man. Now it was a case of, 'You get the fish and the cheese and I'll get everything else and see you back here at the car in twenty minutes no make it ten.' To restore the quality of our lives, I had to learn to drive.

My driving instructor was the most relaxed man I've ever

met. He was also an active Christian. It must help, if you're a driving instructor, knowing that if anything unfortunate happens, you'll go straight to heaven in the fast lane.

'You know, Sue,' he'd ponder, 'Jesus said – *don't let it slip through your fingers!* In the Sermon on the Mount He said – *more gas!*' Apparently Jesus also said – *GENTLY DOES IT WHEN MOVING OFF.* But when it came to moving off, my feet were weak, feeble and disobedient. My natural reaction, at times of danger, is to whip my toes up – ZAP! – until the knees strike the chin. In this position you are safe from snakes, mice, spiders and rampant vacuum cleaners. But it doesn't do much for your clutch control.

Eventually, I did make progress. Gradually I mastered the art of moving the car forwards instead of just up and down. But Peter was expensive. I needed practice – on the cheap.

'Excuse me, darling ...' I poked my head round my husband's study door. He glared desperately at me with the air of a man who had just found the lost chord when I knocked and had now dropped it again. I carried on. 'Would you mind giving me a little bit of driving practice? Just half an hour ... we can go to the bank ... please?'

With an echoing sigh, he dragged himself away from his music. Like most men, he'd been driving since the dawn of life and couldn't remember what it had been like to learn. He was also at his worst when sitting in the passenger seat while I drove. I have to admit I was at my worst too.

'Mind that wall! You only just missed it!'

'Yes, but I did miss it, didn't I? Your attitude is all wrong. I need praise, not criticism!'

'You need to understand – mind that dog! – to understand how the engine works. There is a series of plates ...'

'Shut up about plates! I need you to be quiet!'

'I am only trying to help! – Go now! Go now! STOP! – You have stalled.'

'I KNOW I'VE FLAMING WELL STALLED!'

I shall draw a veil over my first test. The examiner had the austere severity of the Old Testament God himself. Desperately I tried to remember what Jesus had said about turning right into a dual carriageway. I was far too busy to look in the mirrors – especially those little side ones; they were just for kids to vandalise. I really should've taken the test in my twenties at the height of my narcissism.

'Thou Hast Failed,' intoned the Examiner. I was cast back into Limbo, with the red L firmly plastered to my rear, for another three millennia.

When it came to my second test, I had a different examiner. This one was small and cuddly and smiled as if he meant it. But he did ask me to turn right into a maelstrom of a major road. I've never much liked turning right: I suspect it's political. I waited. I got hot. A tiny gap appeared, a gap such as a gnat might have buzzed through. I boiled over, terrified to move. The examiner ticked. Every tick a black mark, of course. Another gap appeared. Another tick. Lava poured from my ears. Another gap appeared. ZOOOM! I was off into it like a gnat up a witch's nostril.

That's it then, I groaned to myself as we turned back into the test centre. I've failed again – even worse than before. I parked and switched off. The car gave an enormous hiccup. We were still in gear.

'I'm sure you didn't mean to do that,' said the examiner, with a secret smile. (Never mind the Driving Test, I thought, will you marry me?)

'That is the end of the Test,' he announced solemnly, 'and you have passed.'

Stunned, I watched him fill in the forms. So this was it. I was in heaven. I was in the circle of the blessed, at last. I had sinned but I was forgiven. He signed the certificate with a flourish, and his name – it will be emblazoned on my heart for ever – was Mr Liberty.

Needing glasses

'Now, Susan,' smiled the optician, with the air of a mysterious conjuror, 'you're going to see what a beautiful world we live in. Look over there! That's the back of the Gaumont!'

I stood ravished, as Cortez beholding the Pacific, silent upon a peak in Darien. I could see the concrete in between the bricks on the back of the Gaumont. Joy. Rapture.

When I was about twelve, I realised that there was more to life than met the eye. My eye, anyway. I was in a maths lesson at the time, sitting at the back as usual (I was quite subversive at twelve). The maths mistress had written something on the board. It looked like a patch of brambles in a fog. I squinted. And conscientious Miss Cox paused in her parallelograms.

'Susan Limb!' she called. 'Can you see the board?'

'Yes! Yes!' I cried, instantly unsquinting and pretending to copy things down. But in that moment, it dawned on me with horrible finality, not that I couldn't see the board – I'd known that for months – but that all the others could.

I don't know why I regarded my myopia as shameful, but I did. I had the feeling that, once people knew I couldn't see, they would flee from my side and leave me to grope my way through the world alone. So I grew cunning. I went and sat at the front. I also discovered that I could see more clearly if I pulled the skin of my temples back slightly, giving my eyes a Chinese look. Doing this for long periods without drawing attention to oneself is quite a challenge, but I rose to it.

However, the Welfare State was after me with its Eye Tests. I approached the Medical Room at the appointed time, my heart pounding. But when it was my turn – guess what! There, hanging on the back of the door, was the eye chart. How could they be so careless? I seized my chance, closing the door with laborious politeness, which just gave me time to memorise the bottom line. The nurse covered my left eye with a piece of paper. 'Can you read the last line?' she enquired.

'P L T Z B D N!' I replied airily, squinting into the mist.

She covered my right eye. 'Now read it again, backwards.' Fiendish cunning, these people. Luckily I found that my memory worked backwards as well.

Time passed. My parents noticed that I sat three feet from the TV screen even when Adam Faith wasn't on.

'I think Susan needs glasses,' said my Dad, who wore them himself.

'Oh no she doesn't,' insisted my Mum. 'She just wants a pair of glasses to make her look more intelligent.'

Actually, Mum was wrong. I didn't want to look more intelligent. I reckoned I looked far too intelligent already. The effort of walking down the road without bumping into lampposts had given me the sort of ferocious frown of concentration normally only worn by Nobel Prize winners.

Eventually, though, I reconciled myself to the idea of glasses, even though in the early Sixties you could only get ones with upswept rims like cows' horns. Still, I was tired of living in a blur. At fourteen, you need to know whether the boys on the opposite side of the road are utterly repulsive or only slightly so. I went to the optician – or as my Aunt Judith always calls it, the optimist.

'Now, Susan,' he smiled, with the air of a mysterious conjuror, 'you're going to see what a beautiful world we live in. Look over there! That's the back of the Gaumont!'

I stood ravished, as Cortez beholding the Pacific, silent upon a peak in Darien. I could see the concrete in between the bricks on the back of the Gaumont. Joy. Rapture.

Going home on the bus, I was astonished by the sheer stipple and grain of the universe. I had, as it were, discovered the atom. Leaves had edges. Pavements were mosaics of small sparkly stones. Only human beings were a disappointment. They had lost their misty Monet-like charm and gained a Brueghel-like grotesquery – with hairs in nostrils, wrinkles on brows, and spots on chins.

Especially mine. Surveying myself that night in the bathroom mirror, I was dismayed to find that I did not, as I had hoped, resemble the young Marlon Brando, but was irrevocably a teenage girl complete with puppy fat, pimples, and, to crown it all, glasses. What's the opposite of gilding the lily? Creosoting the couch grass? Well, at fourteen I felt as if I'd been well and truly creosoted.

I did try contact lenses for a while. They have transformed twentieth-century life, causing many specimens of homo erectus to abandon the millennia of evolution and resume a grovelling existence upon all fours. I've made some really good friends beneath the washbasins of ladies' rooms. In a pub at Porlock once I spent two hours on my knees, examining every fibre of the carpet, before realising that I had, in fact, put both contact lenses into one and the same eye. Then there was the time I left my contact lenses in a glass of water in the bathroom and discovered my father had drunk them in the night. After that I went back to glasses. They seemed safer somehow. So far no member of my family has shown any inclination to devour them.

All in all, I have to report that myopia (or myopia anyway) hasn't been the disaster I feared. Men do make passes at girls who wear glasses, although when the man also wears them, the first kiss is accompanied by an embarrassing clicking, rather like the sound of mating armadillos. But all things considered, I like being able to tune in my own eyesight, like the telly: sometimes wearing glasses and sometimes not.

When surveying my herbaceous border, I cast my glasses aside and revel in the haze of colour, unaware of the weeds, sweet papers and Coca-Cola cans. But up on Painswick beacon, gazing across the Severn plain to the hills of Wales beyond, I whip out my specs and enjoy spotting the distant pinpricks of church spires, and seeing how the lettuces are doing in Gwent. Most convenient of all is being able to hide behind large tinted glasses in public. For, as Raymond Chandler knew, nothing is quite so fascinating and mysterious as the Private Eye.

Mice in the House

The poison was called warfarin. Just the name was enough to scare me out of my wits. But the mice flourished on it. They grew fat and prosperous, opened branches in New York and Geneva; they were not just warfarin-resistant but warfarin-dependent.

I've had mice. If I've seen one, I've seen forty – or was it the same mouse doing guest reappearances? By the fortieth time, you understand, my attitude to these small furry creatures had undergone a subtle change. When I first saw one, sitting up under the piano and cleaning its ears, I was overwhelmed with affection. It was so utterly Beatrix Potteresque. Any minute now it would put on its pinny and start sweeping the floor.

One mouse won't do any harm, surely, I thought. Who was I to grudge it a modest corner of my house, while it lived a life of single blessedness, meditation and washing? I wasn't sure the other members of my family would have quite the same reaction however, so I chased it away to its hole, where I could hear it scampering quaintly behind the skirting boards. No doubt it was busy with its tiny dustpans and brooms. Mice were so clean. Beatrix Potter had convinced me of that, then on one of the kitchen shelves I found what looked like a burnt rice grain. That's funny, I thought, we haven't had rice for ages.

A few days later the scampering had become thundering, and the pantry an EEC mountain of mouse droppings. Packets of biscuits were broken into and nibbled; muesli was ravaged; anything left open on the shelves was defiled. My shy teenage mouse had grown up very fast, and was holding staggeringly successful mouse parties. When I walked into the kitchen I could hear them actually swinging and flicking around in the (unlit) oven, apparently exercising on the bars with all the aplomb of Olympic gymnasts.

This was tactless. It was ungrateful. There I was pouring

out all my liberal tolerance, and they were simply taking advantage and being impossible. A good rehearsal for having teenage children, I suppose. I had to act. But how? Traps? The thought of finding a small furry creature in the morning with its neck broken would seriously interfere with a serene breakfast (mine as well as its). Poison was against all my principles. I settled therefore for the liberals' mousetrap.

It was a small, humane cardboard box. In one end I arranged a quantity of muesli. I left the other end open. Then I placed it carefully in the oven and waited. Soon I heard the chomping of tiny teeth. I whipped open the oven door, slammed the box shut, and carried my prisoners down the road. I released them round the back of the Co-op.

Relieved, I strolled home, entered the kitchen – and was met by the unmistakable sound of mouse olympics in the oven – again. I installed the mousetrap again. Several times that evening – I'm not telling you exactly how many – I carried a boxful of mice down the road. And every time I returned to hear the sound of those infernal gymnastics.

I could feel my heart harden. Liberalism was streaming off me like tepid bathwater. I growled. I spat. I broke a pencil in half. Soon I'd have been eating the carpet, but it was covered with droppings. Next day, I would go to the chemist and get some poison. Nice, gentle, humane poison. The sort that would ease them off this mortal coil in the sweetest of sleeps, dreaming of Gorgonzola. Thank goodness my small daughter, who is interested in everything at floor level, was away with her Dutch grandmother.

The poison was called warfarin. Just the name was enough to scare me out of my wits. But the mice flourished on it. They grew fat and prosperous, opened branches in New York and Geneva; they were not just warfarin-resistant but warfarin-dependent.

The house was scattered with mouse droppings, even though I was vacuuming seven times a day. Moreover, the mice's appetites had extended beyond the kitchen into my study. Bits of writing were being gnawed: they were ferocious editors. They were eating my words. And so was I.

'Right!' I snapped, 'So much for humanitarianism. I've got to get rid of these mice fast – I don't care how.'

What made it even more urgent was that the most fastidious

man in Western Europe was coming to stay with us. He must not smell a rat. Or anything remotely like one. I needed the Pied Piper of Hamelin, but I only got his answerphone. I ran to the chemist and bought the biggest pack of mouse-poison available. This was when the scuttling had to stop.

It stopped. We had tea in eerie silence with the Most Fastidious Man. Un-gnawed biscuits. Unviolated cake. It was heaven – for a split second. And then I saw them. The carpet only two yards behind the MFMIWE was covered with mice rolling around sleepily. The poison evidently took away their sense of balance and their sense of occasion. Would they show a sense of propriety and refrain from actually pegging out at his feet? To say my breath was baited would be putting it mildly. I didn't breathe for twenty minutes.

What would keep my guest fascinated? How could I guarantee that he wouldn't throw a casual glance over his shoulder? There was nothing for it – the conversation had to turn to sex and the supernatural. Preferably in close juxtaposition.

'Did I ever tell you this house was haunted?' I remarked casually. 'By the ghost of a nymphomaniac?'

He was of course utterly entranced. As I deluged him with details the mice rolled away one by one and died decently under the piano.

I still don't know to this day whether the Most Fastidious Man never suspected anything or whether he was just being superhumanly polite. He did leave soon after.

So my advice is, if you see a mouse, abandon your humane impulses instantly. Take no notice of those cunningly furry ears. Think of it this way: would you tolerate a human being who relieved himself in the sugar bowl? Well, quite. Lock up your copies of Mrs Tittlemouse and Hunca Munca, and Get Thee to an Apothecary.

Being scared babysitting

This month is the twenty-fifth anniversary of my most emb-arrassing moment ever. I was a teenager of truly Adrian Molesque portentousness. For a start, I was in love with Dag Hammarskjöld, who was, even then, a dead homosexual. I liked a challenge: I was not interested in clothes, boys or pop music, only in mysticism and international (preferably supernatural) relations. Most important, I was useless at the things teenagers were supposed to be good at – including baby-sitting. And thereby hangs my tale.

I baby-sat. It wasn't a success. For a start, I was frightened of small children. The two little boys in question – Jeremy and David – had been bitterly disappointed to discover that I was not, despite my name, Chinese. Their father was an architect, and they lived in a large and much-improved house in a dark, gloomy, tree-lined road. Next door seemed miles away, that dingy November. In short, it was exactly the sort of place where a baby-sitter might be terrorised by The Fiend.

Frightened though I was of little Jeremy and David, I was even more frightened of The Fiend. I tried to persuade the children to stay up and protect me. But I bored them to bed. I had to face the evening alone. Every time I baby-sat, it was the same: pad, pad, pad ... KLUNK! That was the sound of The Fiend taking up his position just outside the living-room door. RASP, RASP, RASP, RATTLE! That was him sharpening his teeth. In sane daylight I could accept that these sounds were made by mine hosts' battery of domestic machines. But by mad moonlight I knew it was The Fiend.

On this particular night, however, there was no moon and no wind. Still and dark: The Fiend's favourite. Suffering from my usual acute fear, I was enthroned upon the lavatory, when the bathroom door, which I had left ajar, suddenly twitched. And very slowly it closed – all by itself!

Every hair on my head stood on end. Hastily adjusting my dress, I ran for the door – then hesitated. Rushing out would be a major mistake. The safest bet was to lock myself in. Hah! The Fiend hadn't got me yet. Dag would've been proud of me. But how was I to escape? The bathroom window was about eight feet above the ground – just far enough to fall and break your leg without the blessing of unconsciousness.

I climbed out. I hung by my fingernails from the sill. And I dropped – deep into pyracantha (sometimes known as firethorn, but that's putting it mildly). Tearing myself free, I ran like the wind for the road – the gloomy, tree-lined road – and the sanctuary of the Vast Gothic House Next Door. I rang the doorbell – a faint tolling deep in the house – and wondered if this would prove a case of Out of the Frying Pan.

A dapper man in evening dress opened the door, and I blurted out my story: prowler, noises, door, help, terribly sorry to disturb you, etc. He seized a torch with a masterful gesture: no doubt Freudians would be able to explain why.

'Right,' he commanded. 'No trouble. Quite all right. Apslootleh.' (He was Fraffley Well Spoken, and I had obviously disturbed a Fraffley Jolly Drink-spotty.) 'Lead the way.'

I didn't quite like the sound of that Lead The Way. To be honest, I was more in the mood for Take A Taxi Home and We'll Ring You When It's Over. But I led us back to the House of Terror, only to discover that, owing to my unorthodox exit, we were well and truly locked out.

'How did you get ight?' he enquired.

'Through the bathroom window –' I faltered, indicating the mass of pyracantha.

'Well, would you mind awfully climbing back in that way and going rind and letting me in the back door? Only I've got my dress trisers on.'

I stared. Go round and let him in? Why, before I reached the back door The Fiend would have me bound, gagged and barbecued. Would I mind climbing back in? Was this England? 'I've got my dress trisers on.' Who was this fellow? The heir of Captain Oates? (Another of my heroes – now *he'd* have brained The Fiend with one mighty blow of his niblick.)

Miserable, and all too aware of my laddered stockings, I accepted the proffered Leg Up (Leg Up? Was the Age of Chivalry so utterly dead?) and found myself once more in the bathroom.

'Right,' said my saviour from the garden below. 'Now. Run rind and let me in the back door. Dain't worry. I'll be right there.'

Oh well. At least I wouldn't be dead on my own for long. 'Dag – Captain Oates, I come!' I murmured, and bursting bravely from my sanctum I whizzed round to the back door and let him in. He entered with a bound, brandishing his torch.

'It's all right,' he cried, 'I'm here!'

From that moment I knew there was no prowler. But he insisted on inspecting every room, by torchlight, disdaining the perfectly adequate electricity supply. It was, to him, quite obviously, a ripping yarn. As long as the ripping didn't get as far as the dress trisers.

Having established that there was no prowler lurking in a dark corner, he took his leave. I thanked him insincerely. I knew that The Fiend was waiting in a small ball of ectoplasm by the ceiling, ready to unroll and start his games again as soon as I was alone. After that, I went to bed (the baby-sitter had a single bedroom conveniently close to the stairs, up and down which The Fiend loved to pad-pad-pad). Eventually sleep came, but only after I'd heard the architect and his wife return, like angels, talking about ordinary things, bless them.

Next morning I had muesli for breakfast for the first time in my life (remember this was 1963) and told them the tale.

'Ah,' said the architect, 'the bathroom door closed by itself. Yes. That's a rather nice little magnetic system I've installed. If the doors are left open, they close by themselves – magnets, you see. Invaluable in a house where there are children.' And fatal in a house where there are baby-sitters.

Time passed, as it does. I grew up and now I have baby-sitters of my own. 'We won't be long,' I tell them. 'There's a phone in every room and our number is by every phone.

There's also a cricket bat on the landing, and a pair of gallant grandparents in the North Wing. And if you're very frightened, wake the baby: she bites burglars.'

Buying Christmas presents

As we all got hotter and more hysterical, I realised that the Indian rug rolled up under my arm was beginning to emit a curious and not entirely attractive smell. Could it have been made from parts of an old yak, of which the yak, when alive, may not have been particularly proud?

'Listen!' trilled my friend Charlotte over an unusually crackly line, 'I'm going to Antigua for the whole of December, so if you'd like to use my flat in Hampstead, I'll send you the key.'

A wave of uncontrollable envy and bile swept over me, closely followed by a wave of uncontrollable gratitude and obsequiousness. I was delighted to accept her offer, as there was the Christmas shopping to attend to. My husband and daughter accepted my departure with a greedy gleam in their eyes, as I promised I should return burdened with gifts. I knew they particularly wanted two books, *The Self-Organising Universe* and *Frog And Toad Are Friends*. Though heaven knows, their recent presents to me hadn't really been up to much.

My husband had promised me a 'tree-shaped present' last year and I had fantasised all night about frolicking in the shade of figs and mulberries, only to be greeted on awakening with the spectacle of a tree-shaped *clothes line*, for goodness sake. My daughter's contribution to the occasion had been a ball of coloured tissue paper that would, she assured me, kill burglars.

Still, it is wrong to carp. And much more blessed to give than receive, of course. I counted my blessings on the train, though I was, of course, taking with me a certain problem: what to get for Aunt Ursula and, firmly on the other side of the family, Uncle Henry. Aunt Ursula disapproves of everything I do, and accepts her tin of treacle toffees every year with weary resignation. Uncle Henry spends all his time huntin', shootin' and fishin' in lovat-green socks regularly donated by me. This year it had to be different.

I gained Hampstead in record time and, pausing only to dump my bags and indulge myself in the chic little patisserie opposite with a Café à la Crème and Petit Pain au Chocolat, I plunged down the abyss of the Hampstead Tube feeling as excited as a kid on a school trip. Any minute now I would be sick down my blazer. (Memo: No more Petits Pains as they invariably lead to Grand Douleurs.)

In Oxford Street, the shops beckoned with Christmas lights. I dived in. Would Aunt Ursula like a new hot-water bottle? ('I been usin' mine for twenty years, dear, and it'll do for another twenty, thank you very much. You have to know how to treat them.') Could Uncle Henry reconcile himself to a saucy red flannel nightshirt? ('Damn tomfoolery French nonsense. Still, suppose I could tear it into strips and clean the guns with it.') What would he make of a Filofax? ('Filofax? Didn't he win the National in '56?') I knew all too well what Aunt Ursula would make of one. ('You don't need to make notes if you keep a clear head, dear. Remembering things is just a matter of discipline.') Like the elephant, Aunt Ursula never forgets, and that's not the only resemblance.

Three hours later I was frazzled, weary and still empty-handed. I hadn't even managed to get *The Self-Organising Universe*. And if it was so damned self-organising, why couldn't it organise Christmas presents for us all into the bargain? I was just beginning to think lovingly of treacle toffees and lovat-green socks, when I saw it. A shop loaded with curiosities from the Third World. In a trice I was transformed and the fatigue vanished. I disappeared within, reaching convulsively for my purse before I was over the threshold.

I emerged an hour later loaded down with an Indian rug, a terracotta statuette of what looked suspiciously like Nigel Lawson wearing a disposable nappy, and a brass gong that tolled sinisterly all along Tottenham Court Road whenever I bashed it with my knee, which was often. Boy, was I loaded. I was also quite hot. Because I'd also succumbed to an exquisite Tibetan padded jacket, and my only hope of getting it home was wearing it on top of everything else.

The tube whisked me safely to Hampstead, where I staggered into a lift, and was instantly surrounded by a score of fat people in fur coats. Still, it was only for fifteen seconds or so, I was telling myself, when CRONK! It came to a sudden stop. And why? Because a handful of my Tibetan padded jacket had got caught in the lift doors, and had jammed our entry to the shaft. This was pointed out to me by an important-looking man in an obviously much better-trained camel wool coat.

As we all got hotter and more hysterical, I realised that the Indian rug rolled up under my arm was beginning to emit a curious and not entirely attractive smell. Could it have been made from parts of an old yak, of which the yak, when alive, may not have been particularly proud?

In the thirty minutes it took them to get us out, my thoughts reverted guiltily to Aunt Ursula and Uncle Henry. I had entirely forgotten them in my frenzied grabbing at exotic artefacts. Was this a punishment, a sign that I should give away my treasures? At least I had been doing my bit to help Third World economies. Or had I? Perhaps the real beneficiaries of the tribal arts business are lying beside swimming pools in Camberley. Maybe I should auction the lot in aid of the Save the Children Fund . . . ? As if to indicate that I had suffered enough in the way of conscience-stricken agonisings, the lift performed a series of downward jerks and released us.

Next day I arose in sober mood, and after meditating for a few minutes on the inspiring face of the great Nigel, I went forth clutching my purse tightly, and bought the books desired by my family. Then, in a final offensive against treacle toffees and lovat-green socks, I made straight for the Body Shop and bought Bath Balls for absolutely everybody. Even Uncle Henry must have a bath sometimes.

I would give the rug to my spouse as he has cold feet, and the gong to my daughter, who would no doubt immediately incorporate it into her latest anti-burglar device. ('You sprinkle sugar on their heads and bash them with the gong.') As for the terracotta Chancellor, he would preside sternly over my writing desk, enshrining the almost Buddhist paradox that it is more blessed to give than receive, except when the recipient is yourself.

The
Christmas
Story

We're dreaming of a Green Christmas

It was going to be a guiltily Green Christmas for us: recycled wrapping paper, complete with bits of last year's Sellotape clinging to the wreckage; impeccably environment-friendly presents (Body Shop Bath Balls for everyone – even Uncle Henry) and modest Yuletide Turnip Soup instead of the bird. I was just writing *With love from us all* on a tasteful label, when I happened to listen, for a change, to what my small daughter was saying, as she sat on the floor surrounded by her dolls and Teddy. She began with a song.

While Shepherds washed their flocks by night
All see Ted on the ground . . .

She placed Ted on the ground and indeed they did all see him, with the possible exception of the old Dutch doll, whose eyes have fallen out. I hesitated. Should I remind her that the focus of the Christian festival was Jesus, not Ted? But then, it was the religious impulse that mattered. One mustn't be too dogmatic. I had already told her about Buddha and Mohammed and the Magic Snake worshipped by some obscure South Sea Islanders.

'Mummy . . . did we go and see Mary and Joseph once?'
'No, darling. They lived long, long ago.'
'But I remember them!'
My hair stood on end. My skin crept. Was it possible we had visited the Holy Family – without my noticing? Or had this epoch-making occasion somehow slipped my mind?

Get a grip on yourself, woman, I thought, seizing some nuts and twigs and working them up into a few high-fibre Zen-burgers for Boxing Day. Don't let yourself be carried away by the shreds of superstition still slumbering in your soul.

'What did Mary and Joseph look like?' I inquired.

'Joseph had a beard on. And Mary had a long blue dress.'

I tried not to think of all those stories of children having extrasensory perception. Had my daughter perhaps had a vision? Would pilgrims flock to Stroud one day as to Lourdes? Would there be commemorative plates and tea towels?

'Jesus had a yellow and black striped Babygro,' she went on. 'And you gave them my old changing mat.'

Ah! Enlightenment burst in. It had only been my Green Party colleagues Fred and Jean with their baby Atlanta. We'd met them at a Green Party field day at which my daughter had disgraced me by rejecting the baked potatoes and yelling for Space Dust and Fat Frog Ice Lollies.

Fred and Jean do have rather a biblical look, especially in winter, when they appear lagged like hot-water tanks in many layers of Peruvian wool, in order simultaneously to save energy and celebrate Third World crafts.

I explained who they were, and we both felt a bit disappointed. Not that I have anything against Fred and Jean.

'Mary and Joseph lived a long time ago. Long before our house was ever built.' It's always been a slight letdown to me that our house was only built in 1954 – AD.

My daughter plunged back into the origins of Christianity.

'Mary and Joseph went on holiday. And. They stayed in a garage. And. Mary had a baby in her tummy. And it was time for the baby to come out. How did it get in there, Mummy?'

Ah. Centuries of theologians have argued about that.

'I don't know, darling,' I murmured vaguely. 'Ask Daddy.' Ask the Bishop of Durham.

'Little Jesus sweetly sleep, Do not stir, We will bring a coat of fur!' she carolled. 'Mummy! What's a coat of fur?'

Ah yes. Not very Green, that bit. Unless it was an aged elk who died peacefully with his grandchildren around him and had donated his skin to keep the Messiah warm.

In fact, that's a neglected part of the legend, isn't it? Perhaps in some attic in Arles there slumbers a fragment of animal skin, brought by Mary Magdalene, who is reputed to have retired to the South of France. (Saintes-Maries de la Mer is where the boat is supposed to have landed.) We've had the Turin Shroud. Now it's the Pelt of Provence.

'Mummy – is Jesus dead?'

Our house positively vibrates with theological debate, sometimes. It's worse than the Inquisition. It's bad enough having to explain mysteries like whether next door's dog is dead or not, let alone Jesus. On that occasion I'd offered a Buddhist (or was it Hindu?) theory that the old dog was gradually becoming part of the earth, and would in due course, perhaps, blossom forth as a cherry tree, one of the cherries of which might, eventually, be eaten by a bird and become part of the bird. But now my multicultural energies flagged and I took refuge in the attractive idea that Jesus and the old dog were together.

'I hope he doesn't pull her tail,' said my child with a tremor of half-remembered guilt.

'What about the Wise Men? Do you remember who they were?' (No Kings in this house, thank you very much, although I must admit I always shed a secret sentimental tear when I see the Royals all coming out of Crathie Church.)

'They gived him presents,' she intoned, 'because he had been a good boy and not shouted and cleaned his teeth. They gived him a telephone and a slide and a word processor.'

'I thought it was gold, frankincense and myrrh they gave him?' I was rather shocked at her relentlessly high-tech tastes. She seems to have no interest in corn dollies or windmills. I don't think she's going to grow up Green enough.

'No – silly! It was a telephone and a slide and a word processor. Will Father Christmas bring me a word processor?'

'No. Not until you can read.'

'Can I have a go on yours, then?'

'If you're a good girl and eat up your turnip soup.'

I couldn't help thinking, though, how different the Christian story would have been if Jesus had had a telephone, a slide and a word processor. Personally I think it would have made His job a whole lot easier. The phone, for example – wasn't the Lord given to calling people in the middle of the night? And a slide would be very useful for someone who came down to earth from heaven. As for the word processor, well, if you recall, *In the beginning was the Word.* Happy Christmas.

Dogs

'Othello! DOWN!' roared our neighbours ineffectually. I didn't feel that 'down' was quite bold enough a proposition for the dog in question – unless it was the Grand Canyon they had in mind.

They say there are dog people and cat people. Well, for most of my twenties I was one of the toad people. One glance into my vivarium and unsuspecting guests were wont to shriek in horror. I loved toads: they sat in crumpled contemplation like very old men at County Cricket matches. Admittedly, they had their limitations. They wouldn't run for sticks or fetch newspapers, or beg for biscuits, or place their chins on your knee and gaze soulfully into your eyes. Toads do not bound joyously around at the mention of walkies. But then, I used to find all that One-Man-and-His-Dog stuff rather disgusting. I didn't like to be welcomed home with a violently wagging tail and a drooling tongue. (I think this is why I married a sober Dutchman.)

I'd always had problems with dogs, you see. For a start, I was terrified of them. I only felt safe in Italy where they wear muzzles, rather like those baskets they put the dangerous, biting sort of wine in at their cheap restaurants. They say dogs can smell fear – well, it came blasting off me like carbon monoxide out of the back of a bus.

My postman lent me a leaflet about what to do. You should fix the dog with your eye and walk away backwards from it, it said. Walking away backwards became such a feature of my life that I never left home without a couple of wing-mirrors strapped to my shoulders. I knew I really had to get over this nonsense, though, when I moved to Gloucestershire where dogs, along with wellies, seem to be de rigeur.

Friends' dogs offered a chance to get to grips with the species gradually – in theory. In fact, my friends' dogs have often put me right off. If it's not the violence, it's the sex. A nose under the skirt is somehow never welcome. And then this jumping-up business, even when it's only friendliness, is a big design fault. Is your outfit fresh from the cleaners? I can guarantee some emotionally deprived pooch is going to plant his muddy paws squarely on both your immaculate thighs – or, in the case of deerhounds, your immaculate shoulders.

Othello, an ebullient labrador, I remember with a special shudder. Othello was young and his owners – a genteel retired couple from the next village – hadn't quite got the iron grip on him that one would have hoped. There we all were having tea in our sitting-room, when Othello suddenly took a fancy to my three-year-old daughter. He bounded towards her. She flung herself, shrieking, upon me, her jam-and-buttered scone performing an aerobatic loop before landing, jam down, on my one and only cream crepe skirt that I reserve for polite tea parties. My cup of Earl Grey leapt from my hand, scalded my thighs, and penetrated right through to those parts protected – inadequately, on this occasion – by Messrs Marks & Spencer.

'Othello! DOWN!' roared our neighbours ineffectually. I didn't feel that 'down' was quite bold enough a proposition for the dog in question – unless it was the Grand Canyon they had in mind. I made my excuses and ran, clutching my screaming child, to the bathroom, where I attempted to sluice jets of cold water upon her sticky hands and my smoking thighs. As for my skirt – well you know what crepe's like. It shrinks violently before your eyes, like a hurt animal. I've apologised to crepe, before now.

Given this history, perhaps you can understand my feelings when a strange raffish-looking mongrel appeared in our garden and my daughter exclaimed, 'That could be our dog!'

I put my foot down so hard you can still see the dent in the patio. We were not having a dog. They were dirty – unlike cats who have a reputation for Burying It. They were horribly emotionally dependent. They smelt, especially when wet. They kept you up all night with their paranoid barking. They couldn't keep their wretched noses to themselves. We were not having a dog ever, ever, ever, was that clear?

He settled in quite well, as it happens. We tracked down his owners, who said they needed to find a new home for him as they were emigrating. And if they didn't find a new home for him, well ... Oh no, no, no! Not that! I am sickeningly sentimental, and couldn't bear the thought of even a dog being ushered to an early grave. So Ben moved in.

The first problem was to render him toddler-proof. She was doing her best to make him feel at home by throttling him and shoving gravel up his nose. And the odd thing was . . . he seemed to like it. Was he . . . a masochist?

Well, he was terribly well behaved. I couldn't help noticing that my walks around the garden were not marred by any canine sculptures adorning the grass. Was he . . . constipated? A close watch was kept on him, and it transpired he was visiting the spinney across the lane. How considerate! My heart warmed a little towards him. (It was quite tepid by now.) Moreover, he never showed any signs of a libido. He was, as it were, not quite a complete male. It made him so acquiescent and obliging, so polite and self-effacing: I can think of many men who might benefit from the same operation.

He never cringed and pestered, but would lie down a discreet distance away from us humans. Did I say he was a raffish-looking mongrel? That's wrong. He's quite handsome with the light behind him. He has a beautiful smoky-black kind of patina all over his back, and it comes down to just above his remarkably intelligent brown eyes.

When anyone comes home, he greets them by making a low obeisance and going OOOOOOOOOH! deep in his throat. I swear, sometimes, he understands every word I say. And when we go for a walk, and I see his tail waving gaily at the other side of the hedge as he snuffles in the grass, his dear tail, like a tawny question mark . . . I think, you know, he's rather like Odysseus's dog, who waited for years for his master to return from the war, and when finally he came, so altered that none of the servants knew him, the old dog crawled from his kennel, licked his master's hand, and died. Excuse me . . . I need a hankie . . .

Fellow Rail Passengers

'Take the TUC, for example!' the Old Etonian suddenly barked loudly at me.

Now, I'm not one to look a gift horse in the mouth but, depleted though the TUC is rapidly becoming, I'm not sure there's room for it in the bottom of my wardrobe, what with all the unwanted macramé pot-holders. And though I am interested in politics, I sometimes wish the TUC was only a kind of salted biscuit.

Whenever beauty queens are interviewed, they declare their passionate desire to travel and meet people. My own instinct is to stay at home and avoid them. Recently, I travelled up to Scotland by train, clutching a novel in which I was deeply immersed. It was going to be eyes down for a rapt four hours. I was determined not to repeat the mistake of previous journeys and fritter away the time in trivial chitchat with my fellow passengers. Before plunging into my tale of passion, however, I cast a brief glance around the carriage. Reading could wait if, say, Imran Khan was available to initiate one into the art of bowling a maiden over.

Alas, Imran was elsewhere. Beside me was a girl of striking dark looks, a bit like a Bellini altarpiece. Opposite was a tweedy Old Etonian, who immediately pitched a copy of *The Times*, like a tent, and retired within. His wife fingered her pearls with the anxious air of a woman who feared they would be ripped from her swan-like neck at any moment by one of the stubbly desperadoes who throng second-class compartments. I removed the dagger from between my teeth, but she still didn't seem all that reassured. What she needed was an hour's gentle recipe-swapping. Perhaps the dark girl would oblige. All she needed was drawing out. Yes. I'd draw her out, point her in the direction of the Old Etonian's wife, and then slip quietly away to my novel.

So – will I never learn? – I turned to my left and observed that it was a beautiful day. Two hours and numerous stations later I was still looking to my left, but by now in considerable pain, both physical and conversational.

'I love kiddies I do reelly I've always loved them bless

their little hearts mind you they can be a right handful at times if y'know what I mean . . .'

This girl didn't need drawing out: she needed sealing up. My neck muscles had definitely set. I would never be able to look to the right again. Crossing roads would be impossible from now on, without spinning round and round at the pavement's edge, a bit like Clark Kent revving up to turn into Superman. As for the Old Etonian's wife, she had demonstrated her good taste by closing her eyes firmly right at the start of this conversational marathon.

Mind you, it had been slightly intriguing at first, because the dark girl confided that she was nanny to a highly successful actress whose sensational memoirs we had all read in the gutter press. Let's call her Georgia Portugal. We were all agog, even the Old Etonian briefly laid aside his *Times*. Did she really beat her husband with a hairbrush in front of a Spanish film crew? Did she wrestle with tigers on a regular basis? Had she had a face-lift, and if so, could I have the address? Alas, these were questions we simply dared not ask. It was soon clear that our vile curiosity would remain unsatisfied.

The nanny spoke of her employer in hushed, reverent tones, as one might speak of a vision of the Blessed Virgin Mary, compared with whom, we were assured, Georgia Portugal fell little short in maternal devotion.

'She's ever so down to earth you know, reelly, everywhere she goes people open doors for her and everything but she hates that sort of thing she's reelly nice she's lovely and natural Georgia is. She's – you know – caring.'

'Is she? How marvellous!' I heard myself gush. The nanny scrabbled in her bag and out came the photos. It was soon clear that photography was not her strong point.

'Here's one of Natalie and Oliver on Brownie and Pickles.' It sounded like an extravagant American sandwich, but turned out to be a blurred picture of two headless children on horses in a fog. The sort of thing tourists would pay a hundred quid a night for the chance of seeing on the ramparts of some Scottish castle. Georgia was tantalisingly absent from any of the photos, appearing only as a shadowy and marginal limb, as in photographs of the Loch Ness monster.

Then, just as I had managed to yawn politely through my ears for the eleventh time, the nanny fell asleep. The Devotions stopped so abruptly, for a moment I thought she'd died. Then she snored. Beautiful, the sound of those snores. Now, at last, like a footsore hiker lowering herself into a hot bath, I opened my novel. But as nature abhors a vacuum, another voice instantly rose to claim the silence – a voice so authoritative that my book snapped shut and stood to attention all by itself.

'Confounded socialist nonsense!' boomed the Old Etonian, and threw his paper aside. *The Times*, socialist nonsense? I boggled. Perhaps he was such a very High Tory that the lack of oxygen had addled his brain.

'Country's going to the dogs,' he observed. Now that I've seen the light and become a dog-lover, I can think of a lot worse places it could go. My own dog would raise pensions, Save The Forests, and improve street lighting like a shot. But somehow I refrained from such comments.

'Take the TUC, for example!' the Old Etonian suddenly barked loudly at me.

Now, I'm not one to look a gift horse in the mouth but, depleted though the TUC is rapidly becoming, I'm not sure there's room for it in the bottom of my wardrobe, what with all the unwanted macramé plant-holders. And though I am interested in politics, I sometimes wish the TUC was only a kind of salted biscuit.

'Whingeing Johnnies!' fulminated the Old Etonian. 'With their Everybody Out and their It's Me Rights. What rights do they deserve?'

I was beginning to think he wasn't really an Old Etonian, actually. They're all so charming and gentle and civilised. At least, the one I know is.

'Take the Church!'

His wife opened her eyes.

'Harold!' she announced, 'It's time for my pills. Could you possibly get me a glass of water?'

'How is It?' he enquired.

'Worse.'

He rose, and asked if he could get me anything – a cup of coffee, perhaps? Stifling my intense longing for coffee, I politely declined, said that I needed a sleep, and hastily slammed my eyes shut before his wife could start telling me what It was that was Worse.

I spent the rest of the journey behind closed lids. Expensive though my education was, it had not equipped me to read with my eyes shut. I was beginning to understand why all those young people plug into their Walkmen. Next time I'm in a train, it's going to be Mozart in my ears and Jane Austen on my lap – that's the only way to negotiate the dangerous business of Travelling and Meeting People.

Being ill abroad

This is traditionally a season of mumps and yellow fretfulness. It's the low point of winter, when, worn out by the successive ordeals of Christmas, St Valentine's Day and Channel Island daffodils, the entire population can easily succumb to a terrible attack of Pox Britannicus. So I suppose it was silly of us to contemplate taking our daughter for a trip to Holland, which, as everyone knows, is a low-lying rheumaticky place with foreign food.

What's more I'd forgotten the E111. The E111 is a form you can get from your local DSS office proving you are a real person and, if you are ill abroad, it entitles you to free medical treatment in EEC countries. It wasn't until we were actually at Heathrow that I remembered that I'd forgotten it. We quickly installed our daughter in the Volvo play corner, a paradise for teenies and also for parents, since they are not allowed in. This gave us a precious half-hour for a few little adult self-indulgences such as going to the loo alone and buying insurance. Being a Virgo, one of my burdens is uncontrollable anxiety about health. Luckily I could insure my family against everything except Acts of God. (How do they ever establish what is an Act of God, by the way? It's not as if He's given to ringing up the newspapers afterwards and saying, 'I dunnit, it was Me, so there.')

My daughter was already wheezing as we landed at Schiphol, and it was with some relief that we gained our beds, in the Amsterdam attic of some friends, and fell asleep. Only ten minutes later we were awoken by a terrible noise, a bit like a lorry load of coke falling down some steep cellar steps. It was my daughter's cough. She was boiling up, too.

By morning the doctor had become unavoidable. He turned out to be faintly Chinese, and I found this reassuring. If orthodox medicine didn't work we could probably hope for a bit of acupuncture or a herb plucked from a vertical blue mountainside. I didn't find his diagnosis reassuring, though.

'Pneumonia,' he said, folding up his stethoscope and looking grave.

For a wild moment I hoped that Ngu-Mong-Yia might be Chinese for a slight cold. But soon we were racing to the chemist's for a massive dose of penicillin and then counting the anxious hours till it started to work. And boy, did it work. One moment I was hovering tearfully over her hot little head, the next moment, she reared up and nearly strangled me. The penicillin seemed to have given her an unearthly strength. Had she been an Olympic athlete she would certainly have failed the dope test.

Of course it was really marvellous that it had done the trick. But her recovery gave her a manic urge to be out of bed, out of pyjamas, out of the window – in short, running along the frosty rooftops of Amsterdam in her skin. In the rare moments when she slept, I thought of all the awful times in my life when I'd been ill away from home. My brother and I started early by having measles simultaneously on holiday in a Welsh cottage without plumbing, electricity or gas. It did have red squirrels – in a tree outside the window – but I doubt if this was much consolation to my mother as she trudged up and down stairs by candlelight or set off with a bucket to a distant well for water to sponge our spotty brows. When I grew up, I'd got illness abroad down to a fine art. You've heard of death in Venice? It's nothing compared to gastric flu in Venice. I lay for three days shuddering and shaking in a hotel bed. Then I lurched out of bed to throw the shutters wide, and the next time I woke up, the quilt was covered with hailstones (this was in winter). How I longed for England where the weather doesn't usually insist on getting into bed with you. The real trouble with being feverish in awe-inspiring Venice is that it's hard to tell when you're hallucinating. And just when you think you're better, the awful deeply intestinal throbbing of the motor-boat buses can set you off again.

But Venice was nothing compared to Guanajuato. If you

say it aloud, it sounds like the noise the taps make when the water's turned off – which it was, just when we most needed it. When you're laid low with Montezuma's Revenge in Mexico, what you most need is a bathroom. Preferably with water. Ours was elegant, but dehydrated: add water and stir, and we'd have had one, but we couldn't. Hotels, especially foreign ones, don't really like guests to be ill. There's always the fear that others will be put off by muffled groans, and start to be suspicious of the chef.

But at least in a hotel you're paying, which can give you a certain confidence when ordering your seventeenth lemon tea. When you're nursing a child abroad – as we were in Amsterdam – and in someone else's house, you don't feel quite that same confidence. And conditions were far from ideal. The steep flight of stairs down to the loo went WAAARP WAAARP WAAARP in a crazed crescendo as we crept down them three times a night (it was beneath our daughter's dignity to use a potty, of course). And if the stairs hadn't woken our long-suffering hosts, then the loo, stationed just outside their bedroom door, would complete the job. Every time it was flushed it screamed OSKAR KOKOSCHKA! at the top of its voice – a tribute, no doubt, to the artistic inclinations of expressionist Dutch sanitary engineers. On the seventh day, you may remember, the Almighty rested. All I can say is Adam and Eve can't have been on penicillin. After my week of hard labour a glance in the mirror confirmed that I had aged at least two decades.

It was Home Sweet Home and no mistake. I was reconciled to the climate, the snobbery, the dirt . . . almost to the government. With what deep sense of freedom did I make my first cup of tea with my own teabags, water, kettle and milk. Gratefulness is terribly tiring, I find. And of course our hosts had been remorselessly kind and considerate. But how much more comfortable it is to be able to despair on your very own bathroom floor.

Telephones

People would ring and say
'Kamschatka? Drouzhbazak
Chuuuuchulligazak Okozak
ZAK ZAK Flabberjack.' And
I knew it was only my
husband ringing from the
village shop to say he'd lost
the list.

Oh the joys of communication offered by the technology of the twentieth century. One can pick up a phone, dial a number and sing *Happy Birthday* to Maureen Lipman. Or is that only the rosy view of the advertisers? What are our naked feelings about the telephone? Is it the obliging servant it pretends to be, crouching on its little haunches in an attitude of veneration? Or are phones the malicious agents of an alien planet, planted in our homes to bring domestic life to a standstill and reduce us to helpless pulp, ripe for invasion?

As the wise old English poets used to lament, when the phone was first invented:

> *When the kettle starts to sing, then doth phone begin*
> *   to ring*
> *When the chip pan's smoking hot, then phone soundeth,*
> *   like as not*
> *When handsome, strapping milkman calls, then echoeth*
> *   phone through Albion's halls*
> *When woman sitteth on the loo, then singeth phone*
> *   tu-whoo, tu-whoo*
> *A merry note, to senses dazzled*
> *It makes men mad, and women frazzled*

It's not as if communication of a meaningful sort is often achieved, either. You can't pause to smile, cock an eyebrow, or flare your nostrils on the phone – all the little things that make conversation worthwhile. You have to rely on those treacherous rebels: mere words. You can't both talk at once on the phone either – one of the real pleasures of human intercourse. As for me, half the time I can't even tell who I'm talking to. For every silly ass who says, 'It's John!' there's a worse one who says, 'It's me!'

John? I think, my mind racing madly through its dusty archives. Can it be John Jones, who kissed me behind the bicycle sheds in 1956? Or John Price, who threw a stone at my head somewhat earlier? John the shop, John the ex-colleague, John the dry-stone-waller? One of the three Johns of St John's College? And all the time I'm murmuring noncommittal questions such as 'How are you?' 'How are . . . things in general?' 'How's . . . everybody?' While every fibre of my being cries out to cry out 'Who the hell are you?'

They do say that the videophone is on the way. Horror of horrors! It's bad enough getting crossed lines without crossed eyes. It would solve the problem of which John was being tedious, but at what a cost! At present, talking on the phone is the one social thing you can do without having to look your best. And the videophone would offer ghastly opportunities to the Heavy Breather. It's bad enough being flashed at on the common while taking the dog for a walk, let alone in your own hall when you're in a tangle with the vacuum cleaner.

But let us not contemplate such futuristic nightmares. The phone as it exists is far from perfect. Even if you know who you're talking to, communication is often thwarted. Once my phone went all Balkan. I think I was getting simultaneous translation, courtesy of the Warsaw Pact. People would ring and say 'Kamschatka? Drouzhbazak Chuuuuchulligazak Okozak ZAK ZAK Flabberjack.' And I knew it was only my husband ringing from the village shop to say he'd lost the list.

After several days of utter ZAK, British Telecom deigned to send an engineer round. Like Theseus in the Labyrinth, he followed the wire through the bosky thickets of our lower garden, and disappeared in the mist. He reappeared later and knocked on the door just as I was rinsing my hair.

When I opened the door, he gazed sorrowfully at me and sighed, 'Well, love, you've been struck by lightning.' I wasn't looking *that* bad, surely? Not from the waist down, at least. I had my new trainers on, dammit. But no! It was the line that had been struck by lightning, proving that Zeus doesn't like the phone either. I bet it always rings when he's slipping into something more comfortable, like a golden shower or a bull.

There's one thing worse than having your life constantly interrupted by a clamouring phone. It's being Out of Order, Cut Off, Unobtainable. Yes, paradoxically, when the phone is sick and silent, it's as if a pet canary has died. How one misses its merry song! But when I became a mother, the most painful aspect of the whole business was the thought of the phone calling out piteously when I was out – like an abandoned baby alone in the house. So I did what Homo sapiens always do when a machine is making life a misery: I went and bought another machine to take care of it.

Yes, a telephone answering machine. Ours was a sophisticated little job. It had a tiny black bleeper, which, if pressed, cried out WIDDLYWIDDLYWIDDLY.

When we went away from home for any length of time, we took the bleeper with us. After a day or two I would ring home, and the machine would answer just as it answered every call, bless it. I then pointed the bleeper at the mouthpiece and it went WIDDLYWIDDLYWIDDLY. The machine recognised His Master's Voice and settled down for a long chat, playing back all messages received since our departure. Clever, eh?

In theory, maybe. In practice, ordinary everyday telephone lines are not all that good. You may have noticed that people ringing from the next town sometimes sound as if they're being bombarded by asteroids or eaten alive by hyenas. Imagine what it sounds like on a cheap tape recording being played from hundreds of miles away, into the ear of yours truly standing at a street phone in Florence while the local *ragazzi* zoom past on their Vespas. (I reckon Monteverdi's *Vespers* are the only ones that don't need a silencer.)

Even if the line was clear, the caller often wouldn't cooperate. The first time my mother heard my friendly message about speaking after the tone, she thought I was having a little joke and told me sternly to stop messing about and please could she speak to her grandchild? And there were always people who said 'Oh no, I hate these blasted things!' and rang off, leaving a distinct whiff of superiority echoing around their final click. Others, however, were encouraged by the thought of a defenceless microphone and rambled on for hours about their star signs, their divorces and what the Green Party should do about litter on the streets.

But since we've shared a house with my parents, the answering machine has been put out to grass. It's so much more satisfactory for callers to find a real human voice waiting for them. And even if my parents' hearing isn't as sharp as it once was, it gives their messages a crossword-clue element.

A man called John rang about a book(?).

A woman with a foreign accent will ring again next week.

And, most intriguing, and so impossible to decipher that GCHQ's chief code-crackers are still working on it: Gillian Fairyland from Hood House, Peeping (?), asks as nicely as possible when she may expect next month's geese.

Green Euro Candidate facing the farmers

The farmers were mostly very responsive to Green ideas – as you'd expect from chaps who actually work with the earth. As the evening mellowed, many of them joined me in the traditional British blood sport of cursing the government.

June 1989 brings you the chance to vote for your Euro MP. I've never much liked the prefix 'Euro': it reminds me rather painfully of certain hospital departments. All the same, if you happen to live in the Cotswolds, guess who you can vote for? Me! I'm the Green candidate – probably in more ways than one. But since this isn't an election address, I hasten to point out that you can also vote for Blue Henry or Red Tom – both excellent fellows. Or indeed the chap from the Liberal-Democratical-Comical-Tragical-Historical Party of the Middle Ground. I forget what colour he is, but I'm sure it's not half as restful as Green.

Mind you, the colour's the only restful thing about being a Green Euro Candidate. Have you any idea of the sheer terror you feel when faced, for example, with a roomful of farmers? It happened like this. I had rung up a farmer I know, and begged him to get a few of his colleagues together so I could ask them what on earth was going on in Agriculture, how to take the bull by the horns, why the chicken crossed the road, and so on. An hour later he rang back.

'It's all arranged!' he breezed. 'We want you to address our NFU meeting, the first Tuesday of next month!'

I went pale right down to my socks. I, address them? But the whole idea was that I should listen to them! A briefing, I believe it's called. Most of my agricultural knowledge was gained from English literature, from The Farmer's In His Den to Cold Comfort Farm. But – but no. It was no use protesting. I must be brave. Didn't I trace my ancestry through a long line of rather short Welsh farmers, right back to the year 1750? Hadn't I often pored over my Great-Great-Grandpa's account book: '1 Oct 1845: Ewes 50, Wethers 26, Fat Wethers 14, Rams 3, Hogs 39 . . .'

Farming was in my blood. And besides, it was my job to go out and speak to people. After all, I was a Candidate. I must open my mouth and words must come out. Graceful, glittering, Green words. Not my usual favourites: er, um and whatyoucallit.

The first Tuesday came round so fast, I could feel the skid marks all down my spine.

'What are you going to say to them?' enquired my Euro-husband at lunch time, slicing his Gouda with mathematical precision.

'Oh, you know. Er. All about how it'd be better to stop growing, um, cows, and grow beans instead. Much less – er, whatyoucallit.' We were eating three varieties of beans at the time – all horrible. But I did feel I must practise what I preached, today of all days.

A few hours later I was driving to the fateful Hare & Hounds Hotel in the handsome market town of Cornchester. It was only fifteen miles, but twice on the way I had to stop for a pee behind a hedge. Nerves always get me that way. I also noticed an increasing sense of intestinal discomfort: a dreadful gnawing and knotting that went beyond the bounds of mere nerves. And then, as I turned into the hotel car park, I realised. I've had trouble with beans before. They have the power to fold me up, screaming, on the floor. But would this sort of behaviour endear me to the farmers? Or would I be treated like one of the old ewes in Thomas Hardy's classic *Far From The Madding Crowd*? You may remember that they escaped into a field of young clover, and got so blown up with it that they had to be pierced in their sides by the handsome hero Gabriel Oak with a fearsome instrument: 'a small tube or trocar,' says Hardy, 'with a lance passing down the inside.' There have been several occasions in my life when I have cursed my literary education, and this was one of them.

I staggered into the lounge, was greeted cordially by my friend-chairman, and sat down in a comfortable chair. Or it would have been comfortable if Hurricane Haricot hadn't been roaring about in my small intestine. The farmers waited attentively. The room was silent except for the faint rustle of tweed. They all looked ferociously intelligent and terribly handsome: Gabriel Oak to a man. In normal circumstances, I would have wasted no time in falling in love with the whole pack of them. But, unfortunately, these weren't normal circumstances.

'Right, Sue!' grinned the chairman encouragingly. 'Spill the beans!' If only I could've done.

I managed to croak on for about twenty minutes about quotas and surpluses and how the trouble with the Common Agricultural Policy was that it was so Terribly Common, and why should faceless Eurocrats in Brussels tell us that we can't grow Mrs Dora Pipkin apples, as our ancestors had done for centuries past?

Then the farmers had their say. I'm fairly comfortable with Turnip Townsend and the notion that three Barleycorns make an inch, and was rather afraid that they might start talking about hormones, gravity separators and the glucosinolate content of rapeseed oil. But they confined themselves to pointing out, with courteous patience, that you can't put the clock back.

If you could, I'd instantly have put it back several hours – to the precise moment when I'd decided to have beans for lunch. Or even weeks and weeks earlier, when, in the grips of a sudden crazy impulse, I'd first telephoned my farmer friend. Indeed, why not put it all the way back to 1860, when girls had the sense to stick to making butter in the dairy rather than arguing about it with members of the National Farmers' Union.

In fact, the farmers were mostly very responsive to Green ideas – as you'd expect from chaps who actually work with the earth. As the evening mellowed, many of them joined me in the traditional British blood sport of cursing the government. One of them even said that given government support for the changeover period, they'd all go Organic like a shot. Music to my ears. Journalists have been Organic since the invention of print – hence the obsessive interest in muckraking.

We chatted on, and with relief I suddenly realised that all was once again calm beneath my belt. The curse of the beans was mercifully lifted.

I returned home deflated and relieved – a conjunction of feelings I'd never before experienced. All I had to worry about now was whether my daughter had behaved herself in my absence.

'Oh, she was no trouble,' smiled my Mum – a comment meant to be reassuring. 'Went to bed as good as gold. I read her *The Wind In The Willows*.'

Dinner parties

Long after my guests have
arrived I am still locked in
a desperate struggle with the
aubergines. You have to do
so much with these
vegetables before they're
fit to be presented before
the public: slice them,
salt them, leave them to
sweat; rinse them, turn
them over, get them into a
decent school, get their
hair cut, tell them the facts
of life . . .

I used to enjoy dinner parties. Why, I can remember cooking Coq au Vin for eight in a long dress – on a gas-ring in my college room, and all the chaps came in DJs. We smoked Black Russian cigarettes, flirted indiscriminately and felt terribly grown up. Then when the chaps had gone, we girls stayed up another two hours drinking cups of black Russian coffee and deciding which of them were worth seducing before returning chastely to our truckle beds beneath the sickle moon.

Ah, those halcyon days when being grown up and having dinner parties was a thrilling novelty, unlike the dismal duty it is now. These days I can't seem to cook Coq au Vin at all, despite having a split-level, fan-assisted, sling-back, peep-toe pair of ovens that look like something that has just come off the Starship Enterprise.

'Unidentified Flying Object at 180 degrees, Captain.'

'Interstellar chicken, Mr Spock. Dematerialise it, please.'

The last Coq au Vin I made would have been better off dematerialised. It resembled bits of old crocodile basking in pink mud. Croc au Vin. Unfortunately my cooking's falling apart, just at the very moment when the extra pounds and crows' feet are creeping up on me, and I need to be able to fall back on my Bombe Surprise in order to produce something with real social éclat.

The trouble is, being perverse, I ignore the helpful advice of the GH experts who devise menus for whole dinner parties that can be prepared days in advance, leaving you free to mingle graciously with your guests. Long after my guests have arrived I am still locked in a desperate struggle with the aubergines. You have to do so much with these vegetables before they're fit to be presented before the public: slice them, salt them, leave them to sweat; rinse them, turn them over, get them into a decent school, get their hair cut, tell them the facts of life . . .

It is once the guests have actually arrived that the real problems begin: twenty minutes in, I realise that some glasses are empty. What is my husband thinking of? I catch him discussing Beards with a bearded man whose name I forget. Man cannot live by beard alone: he needeth roasted peanuts, wine, and enough Twiglets to fend off the hunger pangs for many hours, as the aubergines remain sulking and unkempt by the sink. After a quick bit of glass replenishing it's back to the Draining Board – but my mind's not on the job; I'm still trying to remember the bearded man's name, the third husband of one of my most recent friends . . . I know it begins with an M. Mike? Mark? I decide to hedge my bets and call him Mirk all evening.

Well, they eat it – all except for the cucumber in yoghurt which I forgot and find still waiting forlornly in the fridge the next day – they eat, drink and are merry, so it's all OK. And there's plenty of talk; in fact, it's one of those dinner parties where there are several conversations all going on at the same time. Mirk is patiently explaining to me the Spiritual Dimensions of Yoga when I catch a snippet of someone at the other end of the table talking about a certain newsreader's sex life. Briskly I extract myself from Yoga, but by the time it's polite to listen avidly at the other end, they've progressed from the newsreader's peccadilloes to the Exchange Rate.

By now Mirk is talking to the woman who broke her collarbone last year. Yoga is probably just what she needs. I make a facetious remark about the Exchange Rate (quite an effort, that was) and then notice out of the corner of my ear that Mirk is no longer talking about Yoga, but has switched the subject to someone in the Royal Family who's rumoured to be gay. What the hell's he playing at? Why didn't he offer me these delectable titbits instead of fobbing me off with talk about Yoga?

By eleven we're on to the coffee, and it's only my contact lenses that are keeping my eyes open. I used to be nocturnal, dashing off my best book reviews at 1.30am, eyes bright in the moonlight. But nowadays I have a toddler who hauls me out of the divine river of sleep at 6am like a determined little angler with a great fat trout on the hook. When life begins at 6am, it cannot continue much beyond *News At Ten*. In fact, my idea of a treat is to let my toddler put me to bed – with a story and a slobbery kiss – at eight.

So the later the hour, the less engaged in the dinner party I become. By midnight I'm having an Out of Body experience: my Spiritual Dimension is tucked up under the duvet, while my body remains propped upright, wearing an expression of fixed animation resembling a shop-window mannequin. The coffee has been drunk, the fox cries on the hill, and the woman with the collarbone launches into an impassioned aria, all about her kidney stones and how they were bombarded by lasers ('Pulverise them, Mr Spock!'). Then somebody recalls the old story of the chap who got rid of his tumour by watching Marx Brothers films – he literally laughed himself well.

I am wondering for a moment if the same method could be used to get rid of our guests, when 'Is that the time? We must go!' is heard from the woman with the collarbone. We all stand up, but it takes forty minutes before anyone actually gets to the front door.

Now, I don't want to suggest to anyone that dinner parties are an unalloyed torture: I enjoy other people's hugely; and of course I love seeing our friends, even if I'd be more comfortable whipping up a sonnet for them than a soufflé. Dinner parties do force one to wash one's face, to dress up, put on a smile and be charming; something we don't often bother with in our house.

In fact, I often think that the occasional dinner party is what's keeping our marriage together, because at some stage in the evening I invariably catch sight of my husband being charming and think how much I'd like to have a mad, passionate affair with him if he was someone else's husband. By the time we've finished washing up he's turned back into a frog, but it's worth going to all the trouble for that glimpse.

Swimming
with daughter

SWIMMING LESSON....

They say the human race was originally amphibious: that we came out of the sea. One day, at the dawn of time, something that may already have had nostrils and feet – albeit webbed – flopped out of the primeval slime and grunted the equivalent of 'Wasn't that bracing!' In my opinion, leaving the sea was a wise move, but, being an Earth sign, spreading horse manure and spreading happiness are synonymous to me. I know a man who delivers me a load of happiness for £15. Yes, I'm an earthling. If God had meant me to be suspended in liquid, I'd have been born a gherkin.

My daughter, however, rejoices in the sign of Aquarius, the Water Carrier. After her bath, she always bales out the bubbles into the loo with a soap dish. Why simply pull out a boring old plug when you can make wet patches on the kitchen ceiling? I have also been woken at dawn with a 'pretend' doll's cup of tea being poured into my ear – like a particularly horrid moment in *Hamlet*. It's amazing how incompatible a little icy water is with the idea of a cosy, early-morning doze.

Swimming has been her favourite occupation since – well, before she was born, really. She was two and a half weeks late, and I know this was owing to her perfecting a High Dive: the Backward Somersault with Twist, because I could feel it. Reaching dry land was a big disappointment to her, and she demonstrated this by lying around like a beached whale for months. She was late sitting up, late standing, and, like a sponge, only really relaxed in a washing-up bowl.

I have several objections to water, especially swimming in it. The first is its temperature. For a swimming pool to be inviting to me, it has to be more or less coming up to a low simmer. I know this is cowardly, but I somehow strongly identify with poached eggs. In fact, once I've completed my statutory five lengths, what I'd really like to sprawl on is a gigantic piece of hot, buttered toast, especially on those icy, grey days that so often pass for English midsummer.

Second, the public swimming pool is so very public; up to the moment when you're safely in the water it's sheer hell. (Afterwards it's sheer hell too, come to think of it.) It was all right in the dim and distant past when I was a size ten, but recently I caught sight of myself reflected in the pool's windows as I walked briskly out of the changing-room, and was reminded of a giant rice pudding on the rampage. As for the quality of the water: eau dear! The seas nowadays are so dreadfully polluted, one might as well dive straight into the lavatory bowl and have done with it. Swimming pools, on the other hand, are disastrously overchlorinated, like the tap water. I don't know which is worse – swimming in the stuff or having to drink it. I suppose it won't be long before a bathing club opens where we'll be able to swim in Perrier, with an 'ice-and-lemon' night for the masochists.

As a hyperanxious Mum, I felt my child's survival was threatened on all sides. For ages I was so convinced she would drown that I never even took her near a saucer. Friends argued persuasively for armbands and other aids to buoyancy, and finally I succumbed. We set off for the pool with two pairs of armbands, an inflatable vest and a rubber ring with the face of a startled frog, all neatly folded up in our voluminous beach bag. With all that life-preserving gear on, there wasn't going to be so much danger of her going under, as floating up and coming to rest somewhere near the ceiling.

First there was the changing-room to negotiate. Already the absurdity of my mission was irritating me; it's hard enough trying to undress a wriggling toddler in the comfort of your own home, let alone in a sort of two foot square sentry's hut, with only an inadequate black plastic curtain to screen yourself; and I'm afraid that at one point the curtain got swept aside and my bare bum stared out at my fellow bathers like a harvest moon peeping between autumnal clouds. Then there were the lockers: you needed a 5p and a degree in physics to get them open, and a further degree in engineering and bad language to get them locked again. Lastly there were the inflatables: I puffed away for hours before a pitying eight-year-old pointed out that you have to pinch the valves while you're blowing, or the air won't go in – or out. (A safety device.) It didn't seem all that safe to me. In fact, I'd become so dizzy with all that huffing and puffing that I saw stars and had to sit down on a bench for several minutes before my head cleared. My daughter, meanwhile, decided to demonstrate her impatience by trying to swim in a puddle on the changing-room floor.

Eventually, though, we were ready. Halfway through the shallow little sheep-dip you have to splash through to reach the main pool, she stopped and blinked short-sightedly. 'I thought it would be bigger than this,' she said in disappointment. You can imagine her delight when we waded out into the real swimming pool; big enough to take what seemed like three thousand toddlers and their parents. She burst spontaneously into an aria of joy. 'I'm so happee!' she yelled, her legs pedalling excitedly like a water beetle's, 'I'm swimming with my Mummeee!' Then a small boy, shrieking like a banshee, promptly jumped into the pool and on to her head.

Now, I've always thought that it would improve things no end if all the worst little boys were securely fenced off from the rest of humanity in wildlife parks. One could drive past in closed cars and throw them a few doughnuts every now and then; that would be quite enough contact for me, until they were about thirty-eight. Although with some individuals, little-boyhood lasts a good deal longer than that.

I always knew that sooner or later she might come into fatal contact with the sharp end of some shrieking little boy and end up in hospital, in bed with mumps, or – most painful of all – in love. And now that moment had arrived: 'Tell the boy to do it again!' she commanded, spluttering and bobbing about, her eyes wild with reckless passion.

I then remembered another theory about the habits of primeval man: that long after we'd crawled from the swamp, we'd go back there every year in hordes, like frogs and toads in the mating season, ready to propagate the species.

As I bore my daughter, screaming, out to the changing-room again, I meditated soberly on our amphibian origins. And you know, it comforted me. So I was worried about my only child learning to swim: what if I was a female toad with five million children? And if their father ever showed up, I'd probably not even recognise him. Ah well. There's always someone worse off than yourself.

Serving refreshments at the interval

I'd expected that coffee, tea, milk and so on would all be laid out waiting. I wondered if there was any chance of a visit from the Messiah, knowing his excellent record for catering for large groups of people on a low budget.

'All set for tonight?' This phrase, bellowed down the phone by my most active do-gooder friend Kitty, had an upsetting effect. I *was* all set for tonight. I'd done all my little pre-bedtime rituals: locked the car away in the garage, bedded down the dog and left the garden tools scattered all over the herbaceous border. Now I was looking forward to a long bath, indulging myself with the last of my Elizabethan Wash Balls, making a cup of cocoa and curling up with PD James and a juicy murder.

'T . . tonight, Kitty?' I faltered.

'The concert.' These words triggered a dull explosion in my chest which was probably recorded by seismologists in Uppsala. The concert! At the Community Centre! Kitty's concert was *tonight*. I had promised to bring a gang of friends and I had volunteered to make tea and coffee during the interval! My mouth fell open and some words came out. 'Of course! Relax, Kitty. It's all under control. We're all coming. Everything's fine.'

I wasn't sure if my mouth was doing the right thing. But the rest of me wasn't turning in a very impressive performance. How could I have forgotten Kitty's concert in aid of the Threatened Tadpoles of Lithuania? At which Montgomery Mastadon was going to play oboe and Stella Seal cello?

I put down the phone. What had I just promised Kitty? We're *all* coming . . . How much was *all*? Could you get away with the notion that *all* was, say, three? But even rounding up a couple of companions was going to be hard at two hours' notice. I rang all my fat friends first, on the grounds that they would be more likely to resemble a crowd but, predictably, they were all dining out.

In desperation, I rang my slimmer friends. At last I got a taker: Sheila. Sheila is only 5ft 1in, and a brunette – barely visible after dark, in fact. But I was grateful. It was a start. By seven o'clock I had recruited one more victim: William Thynnge, a pale youth who talks uncontrollably about all his nervous breakdowns. I only hoped he would keep his mouth shut while the concert was in full swing.

I ran to the sitting room and cruelly summoned my husband, who had sunk into the depths of the armchair. My daughter begged to come and was flabbergasted when I agreed. She may be small, but she swelled the numbers to four and a half. For a fleeting, mad moment I was tempted to take along the dog, dressed up in an old gardening coat, and introduce him as my eccentric Aunt Petronella.

Kitty greeted us with rapture, as our arrival instantly doubled the audience. Mind you, anyone who has ever heard Montgomery Mastadon play the oboe would not care to repeat the experience. But Stella is quite a good cellist when the wind's behind her. I left William Thynnge describing to the rest of our party his first deep depression at the tender age of twelve, and fled for the kitchen.

There was an enormous urn, an eggcupful of sugar, and that was all. At this point I suffered my second minor tremor. A huge crack appeared all along my Pacific seaboard and part of me fell away into the ocean. What was left of me still had to provide refreshment for . . . (I peeped round the door and counted) thirty-five people. I switched on the urn.

In theory, we were now well on our way to hot water. But as for thirty-five cups of coffee – well, frankly, I didn't see how that could be achieved without either cups or coffee. I'd expected that coffee, tea, milk and so on would all be laid out waiting. I wondered if there was any chance of a visit from the Messiah, knowing his excellent record for catering for large groups of people on a low budget. But he hasn't been seen in Stroud recently. Though one of our local Green councillors does bear a striking resemblance to John the Baptist.

I retreated to my car. Conquering the urge to disappear for ever in the direction of the Grampians, I drove at frightening speed to the local late-night grocer and bought coffee, teabags, milk, sugar, biscuits, and – heaven be praised – they even had some packs of plastic picnic cups.

Back at the Community Centre, the sound of a small dog being slowly squeezed to death by an anaconda drifted across the car park. Montgomery had begun to play.

By 8.45, the urn was steaming and shuddering like a power station about to go critical. I looked around in vain for the teapot. But who needs teapots anyway? The thought crossed my mind that we might manage without concerts, too, but luckily this heresy was dispelled by a thunderous burst of applause: the unmistakable sound of an audience released from the grip of Montgomery's playing. They stormed towards the kitchen hatch. The audience, which hitherto had seemed scarcely visible to the naked eye, had now swelled to a crowd of Oxford Street proportions. All wanting tea and coffee, or in William Thynnge's case, curse him, camomile and rosehip. I seized the first two cups, bravely approached the seething urn, and then turned on the tap. Dribble dribble, it went, followed by a seemingly endless pause.

It took a full minute to fill one of the plastic picnic cups with boiling water. I placed it on the counter with a triumphant 'Tea!' But my customer – a red-headed man – stared rather suspiciously at it. I followed his gaze. Ever so slowly the plastic cup keeled over sideways, knelt down at a crazy angle, and tipped small driblets of tea out into the cashbox.

'I don't think these cups are supposed to take hot drinks,' said the red-headed man. 'Have you got any squash?'

The rest of the audience were more amused by the whole scene. They also seemed diverted when the urn, sensing that for one moment no cup was held below its tap, had a mischievous spurt of generosity and shot boiling water onto my toes. Laugh? They nearly died. The audience, not the toes.

As I hobbled back to the car, I couldn't help reflecting that I had done my bit for the Threatened Tadpoles of Lithuania. I do hope they don't become extinct. But if they do . . . well, I think I can truthfully say that I know the feeling.

British bureaucracy over foreign driving licence

'This Bloedij Country!' exclaimed my Better Half. 'It is kompletely krazy!'

'Calm down, dear,' I was afraid he might go back to Holland right away, without doing the washing up first. 'Think of Shakespeare.'

It was like this, officer. We were late for the doctor. My husband had been suffering from a Mysterious Tiredness he thought might be due to ME (I thought it might be to do with me . . .). We were going *en famille* because I could pick up a new prescription at the same time, though I'm not going to tell you what for. You'll have to come and stay and go through the bathroom cabinet secretly like everybody else.

It was 8.30am: the rush hour in our village. This meant the lanes were jammed with tractors, sheepdogs, and Volvos full of children destined for small, chic, independent schools.

When we finally gained the main road, we encountered another obstacle: Road Works; or in this case, Road Does Not Work. One lane only, controlled by lights. At least they were green – just. As the Cortina in front went through, they turned to amber. My husband, a prudent Dutchman, hesitated.

'Go on, go on, go on!' I cried, with a rush of Celtic recklessness. What is worse than being late for the doctor, after all? I'll tell you: going through a red light with a police car – as we soon discovered – on your tail. My husband uttered one of the Low Countries' very lowest curses, and accepted the policeman's invitation to pull in to the side of the road.

'Tell him we're late for the doctor! Tell him we've got a sick child! Tell him I'm about to give birth!' I hissed, thrusting my handbag up my jumper. Luckily he ignored this dangerous, and foolish, piece of advice.

The policeman courteously requested his licence. It was an easy offence to deal with: an on-the-spot fine, a few cryptic little symbols on the licence. Three pips, perhaps. Like being made a sergeant – only downwards.

The licence was at home, so my husband promised to take it to a police station within the next few hours. But when he did so, the police seemed strangely displeased.

'This is a Dutch licence, sir.'

'Ja, I am Dutch.'

'How long have you been living in this country, sir?'

'Five years.'

'Ah now, I'm afraid that is another offence, sir.'

Offence? What offence? Living in this country? Being a Dutchman? No. The offence he'd committed was Failing to Change His Driving Licence into an English Licence Within the First Year's Residency in the UK by Means of Filling in Appropriate Forms in Triplicate, The Offender Being for Official Purposes an Alien of Foreign Origin Probably with Webbed Feet for All We Know, Sir.

'What? Jou mean that after the first year it bekomes an offence to drive with such a licence?'

'Yes, Sir.'

So. Every year Dutch tourists come over here, never having driven on the left, seen a hill or encountered a vicar's wife at the wheel of a Morris Minor. Yet they lurch entirely legally from one hazard to the next, sustained by the glowing presence in their breast pockets of the Dutch Driving Licence. But let them actually settle here, learn how to negotiate hills and vicars' wives (accelerate towards them and don't lose your nerve) and hey presto! Before you're even aware of it the Dutch Driving Licence has gone quietly illegal in its clean perspex cover. You are, despite your familiarity with the rolling English road, committing an offence.

'This Bloedij Country!' exclaimed my Better Half. 'It is kompletely krazy!'

'Calm down, dear,' I was afraid he might go back to Holland right away, without doing the washing up first. 'Think of Shakespeare.'

Within two hours, though, I was cursing too. He had to surrender his Dutch Licence and send away for a Provisional one; take lessons and pass his test before he would be awarded the right to drive alone on British roads again. Our domestic and professional lives flew rapidly into chaos.

He'd take me to the station for my London train – only to discover that he couldn't legally drive himself back home again. Whenever he drove, I had to be at his side: an enforced togetherness offering all of the strains and none of the delightful benefits of marriage.

Navigating through an ordinary day required the most fiendish ingenuity. It was like those brainteasers: a fox, three geese and a packet of sandwiches have to get across a river without any of them being devoured in the process. Or in our case, divorced. The Mysterious Tiredness disappeared and was replaced by the straightforward Homicidal Rage.

But at least the Driving Lessons revealed a few bad little habits he'd got into, which were patiently rooted out by his instructor: hands crossing on the wheel, lax use of gears, violation of speed limits, etc. He had to wait for months for his test, but at least his driving was getting a refresher course. Meanwhile, he suffered the ignominy of what he called his 'Hell-plates'. We counted the days till the test.

Off he went with his driving instructor. I sat at home biting my nails. What if he . . . failed? I couldn't bear to think about it. I was so nervous, I made a cake. (Which, incidentally, had to be humanely destroyed some weeks later.)

At length he returned. I ran out, poised between hope and dread. What had happened? Was it all right?

'Ja, ja, I passed,' he shook his head. 'But do you know what? My driving instructor drove me home, and all those bad habits he'd been nagging me about all these weeks – he's got them all! Himself! And now I've passed the test he doesn't care if I know it! Hands crossing on the wheel, violation of speed limits . . . what sort of country is this? Are you all mad?'

I did not answer. I had a feeling that even to mention Shakespeare at a moment like this was asking for trouble. I went and hid under the stairs until my daughter informed me the storm had passed and it was safe to come out.

I'll tell you one thing, though: we've never been through a red light since. In fact, one day I'll cause an accident stopping at a green one on the off-chance that it'll turn red. They call it losing your nerve. It's not the dangers of traffic that I cringe from: it's the thought of another head-on collision with all that excruciatingly tedious British bureaucracy.

Migraine

Looking in the mirror can be a hazardous business at the best of times, but in mid-migraine I swear I've caught sight of the Hunchback of Notre Dame staring back at me, complete with green complexion and mad, blood-shot eyes.

It's time I told you about my secret enemy. I first met him when I was barely twenty. Since then he's been faithfully stalking me. Hardly a week passes without his sending me a sinister little reminder of his existence. And he lives for the times, now and then, when he steals me away from my family and gets me all to himself, flat on my back in a darkened room. His name is Monsieur Migraine.

What brings migraines on? Well, all the most delicious foods, of course. Red wine and cheese and profiteroles are treats I'm hoping to enjoy in my next incarnation (in which, by the way, I'm going to be male, black, tall, gorgeous, and a real whizz at Maths and Philosophy). For years I couldn't believe that migraine was caused by my eating cheese, especially as Life Without Cheese could not, in my view, be described as Life at all, but rather mere existence.

'It can't be cheese,' I insisted to one dietary buff. 'I eat cheese every day, and I don't get migraines more than every few weeks.' When I finally gave in and went on a no-cheese diet, however, I found that it did have an effect. Before my migraines had been earth-shattering; now they are merely earth-nudging. Though they do still register a frightening score on the Richter scale.

Headachy foods are only one of the triggers, of course. Others include bright lights, loud noises, having to wait more than four hours for the next meal, and exposure to even thirty seconds of a Party Political Broadcast.

Suppressing rage or irritation is a dead cert, too. In fact, it's probably the surest trigger. During my childhood, my brother and I fought like cat and dog. I still have a grey scar on my knee where he stabbed me with a 2H pencil, after I'd destroyed one of his exquisite balsa-wood model aeroplanes in a fit of infantile unilateralism. Eventually, though, my brother left home, got married, and stopped beating me up. That's when my migraines started. That's when the rage started bottling up. Life offered me few opportunities for screaming my head off – apart from my three years as a teacher, when I was actually paid for it. I have since discovered other outlets though. Like Cushion Therapy.

Have you heard about it? You have this cushion, ideally kept in a soundproof room, and you shout at it as if it's the person who's making your blood boil.

'Get off my tail, you ***** ********! Road hog! People who drive like you should be flayed alive! Take that, you ******!' You can punch the cushion, if you feel so inclined, and kick it round the room. You can't sulk at it, though: it just sulks right back twice as hard. My husband's a bit like that too, actually.

Even if you've got your rage off your chest, though, you might still get a migraine from the feeling that you're being pulled different ways: torn apart. Your friend Rhona has just arrived, sobbing, 'Andrew's left me!' when your child runs up yelling, 'Mummy! I've had an accident! I couldn't get there in time! Come quick!' Then the phone rings and an accusing voice says, 'Ms Limb? Didn't you have an eye test booked for this afternoon?' The only way to get this lot off your back is to slip quickly and gracefully into something more uncomfortable: a migraine.

The word Migraine comes from the Greek hemïkrania, meaning half a head. Which is what you feel you're left with afterwards. (In fact, migraine is a one-sided headache: hence the name.) It's good to know that the Ancient Greeks suffered too, I suppose. 'Not tonight, Zeus, I've got a hemïkrania.'

That wouldn't cut any ice with Zeus, of course. He'd just turn himself into a swan and sneak in through the bedroom window. You can still think, with a migraine. But you can't work, eat or sleep. Sitting up is a major operation requiring an industrial crane. And the two-yard trip to the loo becomes an endless trek across a blinding desert that has mysteriously sprung up where the landing used to be. Everything changes its familiar shape and assumes sinister qualities: even one's own face. Looking in the mirror can be a hazardous business at the best of times, but in mid-migraine I swear I've caught sight of the Hunchback of Notre Dame staring back at me, complete with green complexion and mad, bloodshot eyes.

Even talking becomes difficult. It's mentally difficult because the migraine somehow hides your store of words away like a squirrel burying nuts for the winter. So when your husband creeps in and enquires in a whisper if you know where his chequebook is, and you know it's on the sideboard, what you hear yourself say is, 'It's on the hidebound . . . I mean, the starboard . . . dammit, the sidewalk.'

Talking gets physically difficult too. Migraine dries your mouth out and you soon discover that your tongue has been replaced by a flabby leather belt left behind on the floor after a jumble sale. At this stage what you most urgently need is more water, or 'Whore Daughter!' – the closest your parched lips can come to pronouncing it. In fact, you need so much water that you feel the sooner the polar ice caps melt, the better. It can make you ecologically irresponsible.

The ideal way of dealing with a threatening attack would be to retire to a dark room, or a breezy copse of trees, with a large supply of Madeira cake and bananas to keep the blood sugar level up, and a tanker full of lemonade. But how many of us can manage this idyllic arrangement?

Instead, we succumb to M. Migraine, who lures us into bed in no time. When he's had his wicked way though, the feeling of slowly coming back to life is marvellous. In fact, it's almost worth having a migraine to see the centuries roll off you afterwards. By mid-afternoon of the next day you could easily pass for a hundred and fifty, and from then on it's downhill all the way.

Believing in Santa Claus

I went on believing in
Santa Claus much longer
than most children, you
see: almost till I went up to
Cambridge, where I believed
in more preposterous things
such as Neo-Platonism.

For most people this time of year sparkles with life-enhancing memories of children's faces aglow and agog, magic moments under the mistletoe, groaning boards and flaming puds. But it reminds me painfully of a vital milestone in my emotional history: the first time a man let me down. He was an Older Man; magnanimous, adventurous, something of a globetrotter and bon viveur. He took me in, enthralled me, and then, when I was totally infatuated, he disappeared for ever. His name was Santa Claus.

I went on believing in Santa Claus much longer than most children, you see: almost till I went up to Cambridge, where I believed in more preposterous things such as Neo-Platonism. I've forgotten what Neo-Platonism meant, but it was certainly a lot less sustaining than Santa. Neo-Platonism never slipped down the chimney in the middle of the night and left your stocking full of tangerines and chocolate.

The stocking in question was one of my father's bristly old golfing socks. In the era of plus fours, he had used them to cut off all emergency exits from his trousers. Every Christmas Eve I hung this stocking at the head of my bed, awoke at dawn, and extended a tiny, tremulous finger to find that it had become mysteriously heavy and had grown corners (the stocking, not the finger). For a long time I just lay with my eyes shut and fingered its interesting bulges furtively in case Santa was still in the room. I knew he'd be embarrassed if I caught him catching me in the act. And to be honest, I didn't want to get too close to those heaven-shaking gusts: those Ho Ho Hos.

Santa was a little bit too much like God, you see. In

fact, when I became dimly aware that there was a sort of team called The Father, the Son and the Holy Ghost, I imagined Santa as the Father. Why, he was even called Father Christmas by some people – people I later discovered who were the Upper Middle Class. My idea of The Son was a little boy in football shorts, and something terrible in a sheet completed the Trinity.

God and Santa both had long white beards, they both hurtled through the clouds, and invisibly watched you to make sure you were being good. In fact, when the time came that I realised in horror that I was Only a Girl, I was in some doubt as to whether I should appeal to God or Santa to supply me with the missing item.

Doubt, of course, necessarily succeeds – and oft accompanies – belief. Our playground had its Voltaires, its infantile agnostics. Ours was Dan Nash, a snotty little boy who wiped his nose on my cheek and threatened to marry me. Dan Nash sowed the seeds of intellectual doubt. 'There's no such thing as Santa,' he said. 'Our Mum told us.' 'Santa *is* real!' I protested. 'I *know* – because I've had a letter from him!'

Yes, my idol had communicated with me. The previous Christmas Eve, my mother had explained that Santa got very tired and hungry on his rounds. So why didn't we leave him a glass of sherry on the table and a warm mince pie in the oven? I penned him a little note. 'DER SANTA,' I scrawled, with that facility for the written word which was to lead me so disastrously astray in adult life, 'THER IS A MINS PI IN THE UVN AND A GLARS OF SERY ON THE TAYBUL.'

Next morning, after looting our stockings, we came downstairs and my brother found a small piece of paper on the hearthrug. 'Dear Susan,' it read, 'Thank you for the mince pie and sherry. They were delicious. Just what I needed. I hope you will be a good girl until next year. Love, Santa.'

My first love letter! A communication from a god! My little heart skipped in ecstasy. I knew that there was a proper Santa: I had *documentary evidence* to prove it.

The next year Santa left me something extra special – and much too large for the golf stocking. It was a very grand doll's pram, complete with bedclothes. Hastily, I fetched Norman and Jeremy (my dolls were all male) and threw back the pram's covers to install them therein. But Oh Woe! What

135

I saw made my blood run cold. I saw the pram mattress – and it *was made out of material I'd seen folded up in my mother's linen drawer!* My heart leapt. My knees knocked. My hands shook. I ran to my Mummy. 'That material was in your drawer!' I cried in alarm. I knew what I wanted her to say, and it wasn't the last time I was to wish I'd been my mother's speechwriter. What she should have said was, '*Santa wanted me to make it for you.*' Was that so much to ask? What she actually said will be engraved on my heart to my dying day. 'Oh well – it's time you knew, anyway – there's no such thing as Santa Claus. He's only pretend.' My world tilted and went dark. No Santa? What about the letters I'd written him? What about the letter *he'd* written me? Why on earth had the entire adult world gone to such elaborate trouble to practise this deception on us? As my tears soaked into the fateful mattress, the whole Santa charade seemed to me a bizarre act of cruelty.

Now, of course, I've realised the lesson it taught me (apart from Always Tell Your Child the Truth About Santa in Mid-June). It also taught me not to get involved with Older Men who are interested in stockings. They will only leave you in the lurch. It also dawned on me that it was my Parents who had given me these wonderful things: my Mother who had sat up sewing the tiny sheets, dressing dolls, wrapping tangerines in silver paper. I was consoled, as a child, to discover that though Santa was Claused for business, there was always Mum.

It wasn't until I became a parent myself that I fully understood the terrible deliciousness of these secret, loving acts of making and giving. You'll hear a lot, this month, about Christmas being 'for the children'. Children be blowed. The brief delight of believing in Santa is nothing compared with the enduring intoxication of *pretending to be him.* Excuse me – I must go and shampoo my beard.

Resolving to be ruthless

There are times when we all need ruthlessness. Like when our children first start drawing. My daughter's early efforts often resembled balls of wool. She would present me with *Ball Of Wool Surrounded By Flying Ticks.* 'Daddy doing ballerining,' she explained, though to my knowledge Daddy has never ballerined all that much.

Most New Year's resolutions are designed to make you a better person. More polite or considerate, or thinner, or fitter; less foul-mouthed, and perhaps, these days, Greener. My resolution for 1990 is the opposite sort. I want to be worse. To be more precise, I want ruthlessness and I want it big: a size eighteen at least, so that there's plenty of room to grow into it. In fact, don't bother to wrap it: I want it so badly, I'll wear it now.

I often wonder why I've never had any of that ordinary common-or-garden ruthlessness that gets other people so much more easily through the day. Even as a child I was far too obliging. I'd pull my own pigtails to save the horrid little boys the trouble. I've bent over so far backwards, for so many years, to let others walk over me, that I'm thinking of having myself crazy paved.

There are times when we all need ruthlessness. Like when our children first start drawing. My daughter's early efforts often resembled balls of wool. She would present me with *Ball Of Wool Surrounded By Flying Ticks*. 'Daddy doing ballerining,' she explained, though to my knowledge Daddy has never ballerined all that much. Instantly her drawing was indexed, filed and stored in the attic. But the day the ball of wool got eyes was the day I squandered £3.95 on a perfectly good picture frame that could have held a portrait of something recognisably human: Cliff Richard, for instance.

Needless to say, all my old letters go up in the attic too. Not just the love letters: I can't even part with my hate mail. Lt Col and Mrs Corsetts-Obvious of Tunbridge Wells may be touched to know that their letter has been saved. 'We fail to comprehend why the BBC continues to employ you,' they snapped. I wanted to throw it away, but I was afraid that part of me would think I was throwing it away for cowardly reasons.

But the times I most fervently wish I were ruthless are when I have a face-to-face encounter with ... well, almost anybody – especially the occasional employee. Somehow, I can't quite see myself as a Boss. If a lad is willing to dig my garden for money, why should that make me feel guilty? But it does. I carry out trays of carefully chosen junk food and my congratulatory smile never wavers even when I realise he's dug up all the peonies, and savagely pruned the lilies that were on the point of opening.

An elderly Irishman once did gardening work for me and he was given to disastrous bursts of initiative.

'I burnt that awful ol' compost heap for ye,' he beamed one day, on my return from work.

'Oh, thank you Patrick, yes, what a very good idea!' I crooned, saving my anguished screams for after he'd left.

Help in the House often takes the form of the Woman Who Comes and Doesn't. In fact, my experience of domestic help suggests that there are two sorts of cleaner: the one you clean up after and the one you clean up before. Happily, I am now lucky enough to be helped by one of the latter – a girl in a million blessed with the supernatural power to bring dishcloths back from the dead. But in the very dim past, with others, I have struggled in vain to put my foot down. In fact, I find it so difficult to put my foot down that sometimes I wonder if in some previous existence I was an earthworm.

I have gratefully accepted eggy spoons with my morning coffee as no more than I deserve for expecting someone else to do my washing-up. I have grudgingly admired the way Mrs Sproket managed to taint every single, apparently clean wine glass, with a witty little frisson of washing-up liquid around the rim. And I have even paid her extra at the end of the week to compensate for the guilty fantasies I've had that the vacuum cleaner might somehow change into a giant anaconda and swallow her whole.

With strangers, I am, if possible, even less ruthless. I have watched transfixed with horror while a hairdresser teased and sprayed my hair into a kind of exotic Viennese dessert, and murmured 'Lovely! Beautiful! Superb!' when I was thinking, 'Waiter! There's a soup in my hair!' and wishing I could carry it away in a doggie bag and chuck it in the nearest rubbish bin.

There were the Turkish builders who renovated my kitchen. 'How are things going, Aziz?' I'd inquire, too polite to mention that the back wall of the house had collapsed. Well, he knew it, and so did I, so why mention it?

As for the horrors of eating out: I have sat in a sleazy café and forced down every mouthful of the only fried egg ever to come complete with gristle and bone, rather than leave any to offend the proprietress. And at a down-at-heel hotel in Peterborough once, I was ploughing through my salad when I noticed a small but perfectly formed slug sharing my lunch. And believe it or not, I moved a lettuce leaf over it so the waitress wouldn't be mortified at the sight of it as she whisked my plate away. 'Thanks!' I grinned wanly. 'Delicious!'

But those days are past. I'm going to pull myself together. We've all got to gird up our ruthlessness if we're going to gaze fearlessly into the cold wind blowing from the future. Woe betide the eggy spoon that seeks to defile my morning cuppa.

I hope that by mid-June I shall be able to show a pair of dripping fangs to the man who comes to the door to ask if I want my potholes filled in now while he's got a load of spare tarmac on the back of a lorry. And I am grateful that Fate has provided me with the one piece of equipment necessary to practise all this ruthlessness on: a husband.

Jealousy

Recent statistics from the Ministry of Attraction reveal that at any one time, approximately twenty-five per cent of the population are likely to be in love, and the other seventy-five per cent have filled in the appropriate forms in triplicate and are on the waiting list. But there's a lot to be said for being out of love you know. The most undesirable side-effect of desire is jealousy. Even Green Party members can become victims of the Green-Eyed Monster.

In the first mad excitement of love we never give a thought to these dangers. I well remember catching the eye of a tall dark handsome stranger at a party and feeling a flash of desire rend the air. I whispered a discreet enquiry to our hostess, 'Oh, that's only Dave,' she answered. Dave also sidled up to her later and was warned that I was 'Only Sue'. We foolishly ignored these warnings and embarked on a short but eventful liaison during which I discovered that he was indeed only Dave. He did have one heroic attribute, however: his jealousy.

Naturally enough, I wanted to look my best for Dave. How well I recall the frenzied anxiety with which I settled down for the three hours' forgery in front of the bathroom mirror. I was in my thirties when I met Dave and I needed all the skill of an Old Master to transform myself into a Young Mistress.

Guess what his reaction was? 'I hate women plastered with make-up. Give me the natural look every time.' Was this a general observation, or had he noticed the three coats of matt emulsion which I'd plastered over my wrinkles? I went to scrape it off in the ladies' loo, but Dave did not seem to notice. He spent the evening ogling a woman so blatantly painted she could have been hung in the Tate Gallery.

Dave's habit of ogling women was nothing to worry about, of course. I know that all men ogle women out of a dreary sense of duty, in order to say things like, 'How d'ya reckon she got into that, Bert? With a crowbar and a tin of Vaseline?' Mind you, any impulse I might have felt towards tight clothes was always instantly vetoed. 'Not quite you,' was his verdict on anything more svelte than a rippling Indian tent.

Gradually I realised why he wanted me undefiled by cosmetics and wrapped in a sheet. He didn't want other men eyeing me up or chatting me up. I couldn't even have a business lunch with a BBC producer without enduring a KGB-style grilling: 'Where've you been?' 'Having lunch with Rupert Formica-Veneer.' 'How many blokes is that?' 'Only one. He's double-barrelled.' 'The pretentious bastard!'

I tried in vain to persuade Dave that my lunch date was not at all pretentious or lecherous but merely intent on pointing out to me the weaknesses of Episode Four.

Dave was deeply suspicious of the telephone, too. He obviously wished that my phone would only give the engaged signal – engaged to him, that is. In fact, I thought of asking him to record a new outgoing message for the answering machine. 'Hello. This is Dave. Sue's bloke. If you've got a message for her, please leave your name and address after the pips and I'll come round and introduce your teeth to your tonsils.' But it was no use trying to joke with Dave in his caveman mood. He had a theory that all my jokes were the guilty smoke screens of a treacherous femme fatale. Oh would that they were! I have never had such a good time in real life as I had in Dave's imagination.

Eventually I entered upon that magical period of my life known as AD: After Dave. For a while I kept clear of men but when the divine Colin drifted into view, I was to experience jealousy from the other end – the sharp end, in fact.

For the first few days with Colin, I listened fascinated to his account of ex-wife Fran, and of his ex-girlfriends. But by the second week, the jealousy had begun to set in like rain at Old Trafford.

Fran, I discovered, for a start, was actually Francesca. And she had been endowed with generous breasts and slim hips, whereas my own genes, alas, had got their wires crossed in this respect. She had left Colin – how could she? – after several years of torment. And he still bore the scars.

Feverishly I wondered if I could smooth his troubled brow. Or would he always hanker after her? Was it better to be a tormentor? Could I possibly out-torment Fran? Could I even take an evening class in it?

One day, when loitering idly at Colin's place, waiting for him to return from some bar or other, I found his address book. I seized and devoured it. Mary! Alison! Wendy! These names, hitherto so harmless and wholesome, began to shimmer with erotic potential. A Wendy of sinister beauty, dressed in black leather, rose like a boa constrictor from the festering pit of my imagination and swallowed the hapless Colin whole.

'Who,' I demanded on his return, 'is Wendy Pritchard?'

Colin frowned slightly at this bizarre query.

'She's my auntie,' he shrugged.

Colin travelled a lot in the course of his work, and he was always late. If I expected him at eight, at two minutes past I'd start to feel disappointed. At five minutes past, hurt. At ten past, hurt turned to hatred. At quarter past he was lying injured in a twisted heap of metal somewhere. At twenty past he was pronounced clinically dead. At twenty-five past he had been miraculously resurrected and was chatting up a blonde nurse. At half past, he'd run off with her. By a quarter to nine, he was plucked, trussed, stuffed and roasting nicely at 200°C.

Then the doorbell would ring. He'd come! Just in time to save his bacon. And even as I ran to let him in, I couldn't decide whether to make a scene or pretend I hadn't noticed.

Maybe the reason I finally settled for a husband from the Low Countries is that the letters from his old flames were double Dutch to me, as were all the names in his address book. In The Bible it says, 'The ear of jealousy heareth all things.' But as long as it understandeth not, you're laughing.

Selling your own possessions

Part of the business of
buying and selling is that
subconsciously you want
people to think well of you.
This is why selling beds is
so especially humiliating.
You don't want people to
think that you're the sort
of person who has stains on
their mattress.

'You should sell that useless old piano of yours.'

At these vile words from my husband's lips, my hackles rose even higher than my shoulder pads. My beautiful, early nineteenth-century, slightly wobbly, square piano! I'd bought it in student days from a wonderful man who, in spite of being tall, dark, handsome and brilliant, had never ever shown the slightest inclination to kiss me good night. This raised my first uneasy suspicions that Life was not going to live up to Literature.

At least I had his piano, though. I kissed it good night instead. It fell on its knees at my feet at once, uttering a tormented twang. Yes, that was the start of a long and passionate relationship between me and my piano. What! Sell it? I could as soon sell a child.

The trouble with material objects is that they can soak up our emotional outpourings, witness our history and become part of our lives. The cigarette burn on my pretty pine cupboard always reminds me of the chain-smoking Brazilian girl who once shared my London house. I was very embarrassed by the fact that she was a sexologist, whatever that might be. I never dared to ask how her work was going. I was just grateful that she didn't bring it home.

I also remember how she sawed the legs off the single bed I'd provided, and I never dared remonstrate with her about that either, in case it had anything to do with sexology. The amputated bed, the cigarette-burned cupboard, the knock-kneed piano: what a poignant catalogue of my past they make. How can one expose all this quivering history to the auctioneer's hammer or the tawdry For Sale ads?

Because when our sacred objects are offered for sale, all the buyer cares about is their quality as objects. All right, yes, I do see that for a bed to have its legs sawn off is rather a lowering experience. And my husband is right when he points out that my piano won't stay in tune, and there are keys which stick and go on resonating long after you have ceased to want A sharp. Naturally any buyer might be put off by these little imperfections. Market forces, you see.

There's a lot of talk nowadays about market forces and how they are invigorating, or perhaps destroying, areas of our lives from which they were hitherto excluded. My problem is I can't even get used to market forces in the market. Not as a salesperson anyway. I either want to ask an astronomical price to prevent my precious possessions falling into alien hands, or I succumb to a sudden impulse to give them away.

Take the beanbag cushions – an impulse purchase from a colour supplement fifteen years ago. I offered them to the wan and poverty-stricken pair of students who came round to inspect them. Ten pounds the pair, I was asking. A fiver each. But they hesitated and whispered and I remembered, all too clearly, my own impecunious youth (which extended, mysteriously, beyond my late thirties). 'Oh take them!' I cried. The students fidgeted and produced two quid. I accepted it, because I didn't want them to feel they'd been the recipients of charity. These are not the instincts of the salesperson.

As I watched them skip away clutching their beanbags, a warm glow stole o'er my heart, only slightly modified by the frisson of guilt as I recalled how, whenever I'd sat in one of the damn things, my head had somehow been thrown back at an uncomfortable angle with my throat pointing at the ceiling.

For a moment I was tempted to run after them calling, 'No! Let me pay you £10! For the neck problem!' But I thought better of it. I didn't want to spoil their obvious delight at having got a bargain.

Part of the business of buying and selling is that sub-consciously you want people to think well of you. This is why selling beds is so especially humiliating. You don't want people to think that you're the sort of person who has stains on their mattress. And yet, you throw back the sheets and – there they jolly well are. How on earth did they get there? You *know* for an absolute certainty that you've never endured any crisis that would result in a stained mattress. So how did it happen? Just another of Life's imponderables.

Humiliation is, in my experience, inevitably part of selling. I still shudder when I remember the bookcase I had recklessly described as mahogany. This was in the days when I thought there were only two sorts of wood: the blonde, which was pine, and the brunette, which was mahogany. A man with a beard came round. He took one look at my bookcase and shook his beard.

'It's not mahogany,' he snapped. Outrage, followed by horror, followed by fierce loyalty to my bookcase, flashed through my heart. How dare this fellow say that it wasn't mahogany? And so what if it wasn't? Why on earth had I exposed my darling old bookcase to such insults? And who in their right mind would ever want to sell a bookcase anyway? I vowed on the instant not to sell it for £50, for £500, nay for £5000. In fact he didn't even offer me £5.

The most awful thing about this episode wasn't just that the bookcase wasn't mahogany, or that I hadn't known it wasn't mahogany. It was the thought that he thought I was *pretending* it was mahogany. This is why, for a writer who has to sell that most personal of things, her words, an agent is invaluable. I'm tormented by the thought that most of what I write may be rot. The agent seems to think not, or at least she's prepared to have a go at convincing people that it's mahogany. If only she were prepared to flog my old stained mattresses, too!

The wobbly piano, by the way, will be with me to the end. I've hidden it in the spare room. If you ever come to stay, you'll be able to play away all night, in the shade of the mahogany bookcase. Be careful, though. The bed's lower than you think.

DIY decorating

The spring light strengthens, which is splendid of course, but it also throws into cruel relief those little wrinkles, crow's-feet, bulges and blemishes which we would so much like to ignore. I refer of course, to the sitting-room wallpaper. It's considered traditional at this time of year to resort to a form of national madness known as DIY, or, as I have come to think of it, Do-In-Yourself.

I suffer from such bad vertigo that I have to be roped to an Alpine guide just to take down the Christmas decorations. So I tend to put off decorating as long as possible – nay, longer. But last week even I could see it was no longer avoidable.

The walls were adorned with such a wide range of grubby marks they would have given an archaeologist of the future a comprehensive insight into late twentieth-century life. There was even a splash of decaffeinated Earl Grey tea, locating us securely in the late 1980s. My daughter had added to this mélange a stylish fresco in felt-tip pen depicting the Creation of the Universe being undertaken by a girl with ten fingers on each hand and legs a yard apart. The archaeologists would have loved that one. Sadly for them, though, I had succumbed to the urge to Do-It-Myself. I hastened to the local DIY centre.

I had not realised there were fifty-seven different varieties of white these days: each with a Hint of something from the natural world. In the old days there was only white or off-white, but now ... Well, I hesitated so long over so many Hints of this and that, comparing shades and names, that eventually I went a rather subtle shade of white myself: Shopper's White. White with a Hint of Swoon.

What I was looking for was something rather like decaffeinated tea with too much milk in it. That way the stains wouldn't show up so badly. But what came nearest? Barley, Bamboo, Dusk or Acapulco? Scherzo, Pharaoh, Cotswold or Koala? By now I was beginning to wonder if the teeming masses of Eastern Europe really knew what they were doing, heading pell-mell for consumer choice. In my present mood it would have been infinitely comforting to find that there was only one sort of paint in the shops. Or even better, none at all.

Eventually, I settled for Delight. Or, as I would have called it, Faded Old Teddy Bear. Knowing that the old paintbrushes we had were now mysteriously turned to stone, right down to their split ends, I also bought brushes, a roller, and most important of all, a tube of sweets.

Decorating is a real giveaway, vis-à-vis human character. Before opening a tin of paint, anyone with a grain of sense would dress from head to foot in old clothes, cover furniture and floor with dust sheets, and lay in a good supply of rags. Some people would even wash down the walls, strip off the old wallpaper and sand down the woodwork for reglossing. I will never be one of those people.

My only concession to decorating is to take my contact lenses out. Splashes of paint are fatal to contact lenses, giving a pebbledash feel to the inner eyelid which is not terribly welcome. And I find I paint with a lot more pleasure and confidence when I can't actually see what it is that I'm doing.

In fact – and this is really important, it's the first Good Housepainting tip I've conveyed in three years' writing for this august organ – the best way to paint your ceiling is *not to look up at all*. Stand on the table, raise your roller and lower your gaze. This entirely avoids backache, covering your face with a light drizzle, and falling off the table. You can glance up after each little bit, if you must, to see how you're doing, but the really adventurous need never look up at all.

After two hours of heroic rollering, I had covered the ceiling, and indeed the floor, with Delight. I'd also incorporated three spiders' webs, complete with an assortment of dead spiders and flies, into the corners to provide a little texture. I had reached the end of the tube of sweets, and of the afternoon radio play.

After the ceiling, all the rest was downhill. I should have stripped the wallpaper off, really. I had thought that a nice dollop of Delight would sort of stick the flapping bits down again, but it didn't. Not that I cared. I was caring less and less about anything, as the hours passed. By the time I reached the fourth wall I didn't even care that there was paint all over my shoes and that with every step, I was tracing little tracks into the carpet, like some poor wounded animal looking for a comfortable place in which to lie down and die.

As I lay, exhausted, on the sofa, staring up at the little bit I'd missed, and waiting for a St Bernard to come lumbering up with a barrel of decaffeinated Earl Grey round his neck, I made an awful discovery. I wasn't all that keen on Delight, after all. It was not so much Faded Old Teddy Bear as Aged Polecat. But once it's covered in Ready Brek and felt-tip pen, well, I think I could become quite fond of it. Although I'm sure if I go back in five years hoping to get some more, I'll be told that Delight has been discontinued. Ah well. Serve it right.

Going to the circus

The first act was Raimondo
and His Flashing Balls. He
entered the ring on top of a
flashing ball, his feet
pattering wildly like a
woman in a very tight skirt.
Then he whizzed round the
ring with a flashing ball on
each outstretched arm. It
was stylish. It was clever.
And definitely not
humiliating. Though I
couldn't imagine Prince
Philip doing it without some
loss of dignity.

Isn't parenthood strange? You spend the first eighteen months patiently encouraging your children to talk, and the next three years yelling at them to shut up. You glow with pride when at last they get the hang of reading, and then you realise they'll be able to read adverts and billboards and get cravings for inconvenient things.

'Mummy! There's a circus poster! Can we go to the circus? Please, please, please, please, please, please!' I couldn't complain really. I'd spent so many years trying to get her to say *please*. But a circus . . . ?

Circuses (or is it Circe? Or was she an Ancient Greek lady in the bacon business?) are a little bit, well, a little bit too Ancient Greek nowadays. The animal rights movement has made us all think about how much better it is for animals to roam free in their natural environments than to be tamed and trained and humiliated by man. I sometimes wonder where our dog would rather be: prowling out on the prairie or sprawled on our carpet waiting for the odd morsel of Jaffa Cake to come his way. I sometimes think he thinks *he's* tamed and trained and humiliated *us*.

'Please Mummy! The circus! PLEASE!' The imploring continued.

'Oh, all right then.'

After all, it would be interesting to see just how far circuses have evolved from travelling menageries into People Shows, in which human beings commit acts of staggering recklessness very high above one's head. I suffer quite badly from vertigo. But I was prepared – not for the first time in my life – to close my eyes and think of England. There was also the feeling that my child should experience a live show – the roar of the greasepaint, the smell of the crowd – before entertainment disappears with a despairing gurgle into the compact disc and video.

So off we went. It was a day of intense cold, but I was encouraged by the promise of a Heated Big Top. When we joined the seventeen other hardy souls who were the audience, I began to realise that heat rises, and that though the Big Top might be heated, the Big Bottom certainly wasn't. Thank God I was wearing my thermonuclear underwear.

My husband bought some popcorn, which cheered us up. It's like eating polystyrene. You feel that if you eat much more you'll become one of those sag bags that were so fashionable in the Seventies.

The first act was Raimondo and His Flashing Balls. He entered the ring on top of a flashing ball, his feet pattering wildly like a woman in a very tight skirt. Then he whizzed round the ring with a flashing ball on each outstretched arm. It was stylish. It was clever. And definitely not humiliating. Though I couldn't imagine Prince Philip doing it without some loss of dignity.

Now it was the anacondas. At least I think they were anacondas. They were big fat snakes anyway. A girl in sparkly tights got one out of a box and paraded round the ring with it draped over her shoulders, a bit like an old-fashioned fox stole. I prayed that it was not going to slither out of the ring and devour my child.

'What's it going to do, Mummy?'

'Er . . . I'm not sure.'

After three circuits of the ring, the girl in sparkly tights struck a melodramatic pose and . . . guess what? *She popped the snake's head into her mouth!* I have never screamed in public before, unless you count teaching. When I'd recovered though, I had some comforting thoughts.

'That wasn't really animal training, was it?' I whispered. 'I mean, it was more outstanding bravery on the girl's part.'

I then spent quite a few minutes wondering which I would hate most: a snake's head in my mouth or my head in a lion's. Perhaps there are consolations, after all, in the dull life of a freelance writer. The only unusual thing I am required to put in my mouth in the course of the working day is the end of a poison pen.

Next came a girl in – well, very little, actually: a sort of single sparkle strategically placed. She shinned up a rope until she was right in the apex of the Big Top. I got vertigo. I was sure I was somehow going to fall upwards and join her. I closed my eyes.

She hung from a thong by her teeth, and whirled round and round. Or so my family told me. My daughter was transfixed. So was her Dad. I think he was hoping that with all this whirling the girl might lose her sparkle. 'Tell me when she's safely on the ground again,' I hissed. I was sure the thong would snap, and she would plummet to her death on the sawdust. I was beginning to appreciate the safety of compact discs. Nobody ever actually died on a compact disc, did they?

Then it was the ponies. 'They look well fed and happy,' I observed as they trotted round the ring, pausing occasionally to bow, turn, and retrieve sugar lumps from the trainer's mouth. 'And the trainer's got a kind face. He looks a bit like my Dad.' 'So did Hitler,' remarked my husband: rather unnecessarily, I thought.

Of course the clowns were wonderful. Mind you, I've never quite got over a childhood conviction that instead of being funny, clowns are actually rather mad and frightening. So that my daughter wouldn't be frightened, I laughed – till I choked. 'Squeak like that again, Mummy! Make that funny noise and go all red and cry, pleeeeeease!'

So we slunk home – furtively, with my thermonuclear undies pulled right up over my head, in case we met any of my Green Party friends. And on the way I had the consoling thought that even if circuses finally disappear forever we will always have the thrills, the spills, and the cascading buckets of family life to keep us entertained.

Trying to get motivated to get up and go

I'm not sure exactly what a full power-shower head is, but I wouldn't like to meet one on a dark night. My shower head resembles a rusty watering-can rose, from which a fitful dribble will eventually emerge if the wind is in the west.

National Motivation Week takes place in May. 'Cripes!' I thought, studying the promotional bumph. 'This could be what I've been waiting for all my life.' Its aim is to get us all to cultivate our Get Up and Go, and it's supported by celebrities like Michael Fish, Cliff Richard and Jeffrey Archer – three of my absolute heart-throbs. What! Was it possible that in a mere week, I could discover in myself unsuspected reserves of the pzazz, the sheer wow I so admire in Michael, Cliff and Jeffrey?

How to get up and go, it said. I read on eagerly. *Have a vital reason to get out of bed*. Now, this is not a problem. My vital reason for getting out of bed is usually that my young daughter is pouring a doll's cupful of cold 'ea up my nose. I felt pleased, though. Already I was doing quite well. Perhaps I had more Get Up and Go than I thought.

But wait! *Lift the spirits before rising*. To be honest, to lift my spirits before rising requires the engineering genius of Red Adair. *Wake up earlier on a Monday morning, be enthusiastic, and as you wake up, say 'I love Mondays.'* I tried this, honestly, but somehow, 'I love Mondays' came out as, 'Oh hell, where's the aspirins?' The thought of Jeffrey Archer springing out of bed crying, 'I love Mondays!' made me feel deeply ashamed.

Get the circulation going. Get a full power-shower head and use it full force, tingling and zipping up the circulation. I'm not sure exactly what a full power-shower head is, but I wouldn't like to meet one on a dark night. My shower head resembles a rusty watering-can rose, from which a fitful dribble will eventually emerge if the wind is in the west.

On the way to work, smile at everybody you meet. Ah. Now here's a problem. My route to work goes as follows: leave kitchen, turn right, proceed to end of corridor, go through sitting room and thence to study. I set out with an absolutely dazzling smile plastered across my face, but was only able to bestow it on the barometer and the dog before it froze, cracked, and dropped off. The smile, not the barometer. As for the dog, it bristled. Honestly! I get no support round here. I bet Michael Fish's dog doesn't bristle when he smiles at it on Mondays. Or do I mean Michael Dog's fish?

Is your brain getting enough oxygen? Plainly not. I think the problem is that it is getting too many custard creams instead. I've noticed during the past year that my brain has gradually given up on Get Up and Go. It inclines more to Sit Down and Stay. *Give your brain positive thoughts as against negative thoughts.* 'Listen, brain!' I said, giving it something positive to chew on. 'Get up and go, right? Like Cliff Richard. Have you got enough oxygen? Would you like to listen to a personal development cassette, as recommended by National Motivation Week?' My brain didn't answer. It went right on lying on its sofa.

An awful thought crossed my mind. Was I . . . apathetic? Luckily, National Motivation Week has drawn up a checklist so you know what the telltale signs are. An apathetic person *Wears curlers in front of the spouse.* Disgusting! You can't for a moment imagine Jeffrey Archer doing that, can you? *Makes love on set day, time, place and routine.* Preposterous! *Has given up on the negligée routine.* This flummoxed me. And then the ghastly truth dawned: I wasn't just apathetic enough to have given up on the negligée routine, I was so apathetic I'd never even got into the habit in the first place. I was sobered, but inspired, at the thought of Cliff, Michael and Jeffrey climbing into their Janet Reger every night.

I certainly needed to clean up my act. *Make sure that the clothes you are wearing look successful.* Summoning up extraordinary courage, I cast my eyes down. I was wearing an appropriately named sweatshirt adorned with toast crumbs. I wasn't sure if my ensemble could quite be described as successful. My clothes somehow are the sort that always attract passing door-handles and stray nails. My sweaters, I suspect, were all knitted in Ripping Yarns.

159

People often judge a person by their footwear. At this, my fears began to be roused. I do see that what a person wears on their feet is infinitely more important than what they say or do, or how they treat others. For months now I've worn a pair of Ecco boots – the low, flat, lace-up sort – and I now find I can get to work in the mornings without collapsing with cramp by the barometer. But does this mean people are going to think I'm a low, flat, laced-up sort of person? And if we should judge a person by what's on their feet, why does Mrs Thatcher go on wearing shoes that hurt? Still, at least the dear lady is not short of Get Up and Go.

Happiness does not come from possessions, cars, televisions, boats. Happiness only really comes from people. As people make happiness, create a home that people love to come and visit. Ah! How true! Words of almost Oriental wisdom. But erring disciple Su-Lim falls far short. I have managed to organise Living in a House, but I'm not sure I shall ever get the hang of pink frills and candlewick enough to Create a Home. Nor am I entirely convinced that happiness results from people coming to visit. In my experience the moment of most intense happiness is when you're waving them goodbye.

But at this point I slid the National Motivation Week literature into a drawer. It was plain I could never live up to these ideals. Alas, I was doomed to disappoint Michael, Jeffrey and Cliff. I was, it seems, chronically apathetic. Still . . . er . . . well . . . never mind, eh?

Videoing the birthday party

I went outside. The sun, unimpeded by all that ozone, was bouncing off Cotswold stone like a whole athletics team of angels. But the camera sulked. Not Enough Light, it insisted, like a toddler locked into its own infuriating logic. 'Well, how much do you want?' I screamed, just resisting the temptation to hurl it onto the flagstones. It was at this moment that I noticed the lens cap was still on.

All over Europe, the Party is losing its grip: dissolving, reforming, suffering agonies and anxieties of self-doubt. But in our house The Party is safe and well. I am desperately attempting to introduce new ideas, but in vain. The hardliners, led by my daughter, insist that it must all go on as always, when it comes to The Party. The Birthday Party, that is.

There must be Dead Lions (not very ecological, that game), there must be take-home bags, there must be balloons on the gate, even though we all know they go pop against the hawthorn long before the first guest has arrived. 'Come on,' I urged enthusiastically. 'Let's be more imaginative. Let's do things differently this year.'

I got a book called something like *How To Give A Children's Party And Survive To Tell The Tale*. It informed me that if I were any use as a mother, I would have been hard at work for weeks making gingerbread dinosaurs and a cake shaped like a real working nuclear power station. But it did offer one idea which really appealed to me. 'Video your party,' it suggested. 'Hire a Camcorder.'

This was it – my chance to introduce an element of The New without totally upsetting the sacred rituals of The Party. I rushed to the video-hire place. 'It's very simple,' said the woman. 'This is the lead to the charger, this is the lead to link you up to your VCR to transfer the tape, and this is your lead to use if your TV hasn't got a Euro-adaptor.' Or something like that. I staggered out, my bag so bursting with leads I looked like a jellied-eel salesman.

The morning of the party dawned fair and bright. The

cake was collected, the jellies shimmering like the domes of Red Square. I had hidden little boxes of Smarties all round the house, only trodden on one, and made a list of games. All I had to do now was learn to use the video Camcorder. (That's modern for camera, by the way.)

I placed it stylishly on my shoulder, as I had seen people do on the TV news, squinted down the viewfinder, and pressed the ON button. The screen remained blank, but a petulant little sign flashed up, complaining that there was Not Enough Light!

'Draw back the curtains!' I cried. 'Switch on the lights!' Still Not Enough Light. 'Right – into the kitchen!' The kitchen's the lightest room in our house, and this was a sunny Saturday – the sunniest day of the week. Not Enough Light, insisted the Camcorder. Not Enough Light? It was so bright, it made my eyeballs scream.

I went outside. The sun, unimpeded by all that ozone, was bouncing off Cotswold stone like a whole athletics team of angels. But the camera sulked. Not Enough Light, it insisted, like a toddler locked into its own infuriating logic. 'Well, how much do you want?' I screamed, just resisting the temptation to hurl it on to the flagstones. It was at this moment that I noticed the lens cap was still on.

Still, this was quite a competent beginning, compared with later attempts to Connect Camcorder to VCR and Obtain Pictures on TV Screen. Ten minutes of mystified groping persuaded me that my TV hadn't got a Euro-adaptor, or if it had, it wasn't going to show me till after we were married. So I had to link the camera to the TV with a network of leads going via a little black box. As I went steadily more crazy, and the leads knitted themselves into a sort of ghastly leatherette belt, it did cross my mind that if I were to explode, they would at least be able to retrieve the little black box and rerun my last frantic moments.

Then the children arrived, and after a greedy scrum of present opening we settled into Musical Statues. I didn't expect to video this, since it was as much as I could do to operate the early 1970s record player and dispense deeply unpopular liquorice sweets to winners and losers alike.

'Right then, we'll have tea now!' announced one authoritative little girl, and they all stormed off to the kitchen, leaving

163

me with forty seconds of Benny Goodman all to myself – the best moment of the afternoon. I followed to the kitchen, entered the fray and seized the camera. This was it. As the children ate (in a strange Trappist silence), I crept around, treading on crisps and trailing all the leads behind me like dreadlocks, only a lot less stylish.

Somehow we never got around to looking at the video there and then. It all ended with a series of animal races across the sitting-room floor. I ran out of slow-moving animals quite soon. 'This time I want you to be a . . .' Twelve pairs of eyes fixed trustingly on me. What further delight was Betsy's Mummy going to produce? What animals were there left? 'Be an – an axolotl. On your marks, get set, go!'

The videotape itself could not have been more avant-garde: a two-minute close-up of Sharon's left nostril, followed by a detailed exhibition of Mark doing something unfortunate, then a strange looming plunge into the cake, then a merciful slide into electronic drizzle.

Was it worth all the trouble? Oh goodness me, *yes*. The Camcorder was a blessing. The unspeakable awfulness of having to make the video meant that I hardly noticed the unspeakable awfulness of having to give the party at all.

Having a cold

When you've got a cold, the bugs have so many tempting little corridors to run down, like in a spy movie. 'Where are you Igor?' 'Halfway down the right sinus. Just planting a little explosive device – then I'm off to the left eardrum to inflict a bit of tickling-torture.'

Ah! August! Time to relax, I thought, breathing deeply and, in theory, feeling more wonderful than at any other time of year. But, wait a minute, what was this . . . ?

I couldn't believe it: I was getting a cold. The sun was blazing fiercely down, the cricket commentators were well into their third chocolate cake, and suddenly my throat wasn't a throat any more, but a hedgehog sanctuary. Or maybe a hawthorn hedge. Just possibly even a hedgehog sanctuary in a hawthorn hedge.

I h'med. I hawed. I hacked. I remembered what hacking coughs are for: to hack your way, machete-like, through the hawthorn. But it didn't work. The thorns sprang up with renewed vigour, like the prickly forest around Snow White's castle.

I made myself one of those effervescent vitamin C drinks. Boy, do they effervesce. My mother came into the kitchen while it was still fizzing and cocked her ever-alert ear. 'What's that?' she asked. 'Is Dad mowing the lawn at this time of night?' The vitamin C had some effect, though. By bedtime the monstrous prickles in my throat had dwindled to a slight tickle.

However, after the first three and a half hours of tossing and turning, I would happily have welcomed back the monstrous prickle if it meant getting rid of the slight tickle. Its very smallness made it somehow more irritating. It was like having a crumb in the bed, or a piece of grit inside your shoe.

I coughed. I swallowed. I swallowed harder. I swallowed with a terrific gulp, but the tickle was still there. From the darkness the illuminated fingers of the clock twinkled cheerily at me: 02.49. Cough-cough, swallow-swallow, tickle-tickle. Cough sweets had no effect except to stick my teeth together. At 4am I got up and made myself a piece of scratchy toast, in the hope of sort of ripping the tickle out by the roots as the toast went down.

At 07.00 precisely, the hour at which night might be said officially to have ended, the tickle disappeared. But something even more ghastly had come in its place. My entire head had filled up with porridge.

'Good bordig!' I greeted my family. They did not look particularly pleased to see me. Indeed one of the worst things about having a cold is that one becomes thoroughly repugnant. And though your nearest and dearest can flee from your presence as from a B-movie monster, you can't. You're stuck with yourself, when what you really long for is an amicable, if temporary, separation.

Feed a cold, the saying goes. I consoled myself with greed. I had a Barbite sadwich ad thed a barbalade sadwich and three cups of Lapsag Souchog. Then two bore vitabid C pills. At least, I think that's what I had. I can't be completely sure. Everything had started to taste of cardboard – except me. I tasted of very old Camembert, with a dash of salt and vinegar.

'Tibe to go to school,' I told my daughter. 'Cobe od! Get a bove od!' 'Talk properly, Mummy!' she complained, terrified that I would cause embarrassment in the playground by not being fully in control of my m's. But my head-cold voice was nothing compared with what followed: my laryngitis voice.

In my experience, laryngitis can turn a speaking engagement into a squeaking engagement. On this occasion I had promised to talk to Chipping Wurzel Green Party about The End of the Cold War. But I wasn't so sure the Cold War had ended after all. Perhaps it had started up again in my very own head.

I had to cancel. I lifted the phone and dialled a Chipping Wurzel number. 'H..l...!' I whispered. 'Th.. ..s. ..S..Limb.' 'Hello?' asked the woman in charge. 'Is there anyone there? Hello? Hello?' 'It's... s..ry... l...ryng...t...s.' 'This is an awful line,' she said. 'Would you mind ringing back?'

A few hours later, I suddenly acquired a voice. But it

167

was somebody else's. He was 6ft 2in, weighed 15 stone, and I think he came from somewhere in the Deep South. I felt rather like a medium being possessed by a spirit guide. The real me had Passed Over into the Silent World – the world of laryngitis. But my Spirit Guide could speak for me. 'Me Sioux,' he boomed gravely. 'Sioux no come to meeting. Sioux got squaw throat.'

I've always thought it was a big evolutionary mistake to have our ear, nose and throat tubes all connected. I thought so first when as a shivering little mite I was pushed by a rough boy into the swimming pool. Noses were not designed, surely, to serve as drainpipes for chlorine. And I couldn't just smell it and taste it – I could hear it.

When you've got a cold, the bugs have so many tempting little corridors to run down, like in a spy movie. 'Where are you Igor?' 'Halfway down the right sinus. Just planting a little explosive device – then I'm off to the left eardrum to inflict a bit of tickling-torture.'

It was at this point that I went down on my knees to the doctor and begged for penicillin. He looked very doubtful, and scratched his ear. (Heavens! Had Igor leapt across the intervening space and invaded him?) But eventually he reached for his prescription pad – after I'd lied about how long I'd been ill.

A few days later, I bent down to pull up a weed, and it happened. My ears popped, my throat cleared: fresh air suddenly sneaked deliciously through my sinuses for the first time for three weeks. I smelt a newly mown lawn, and remembered it was summer.

I am now miraculously myself again. Apart from the red nose, that is. Never mind, though. It matches my roses.

Posh hotels

Once I was safely in my
room, what I wanted most
of all was a snooze. I wasn't
quite in the arms of
Morpheus, though we were
definitely eyeing each
other up, when an
imperious knock on the
door catapulted me
from under my quilt,
like a mushroom leaving a
pancake that has been hit
with a mallet.

Staying in hotels can be an embarrassing experience. In no other situation are one's private rituals – having a bath, going to bed – conducted in such close proximity to the general public. In some hotels I've stayed at, the rooms seem to be separated only by a thin sheet of cardboard. Not that I mind. I'm not proud. Indeed, normally I would install myself at Hazeldene Villa Guest House and enjoy making endless free cups of tea all evening using the same, increasingly exhausted, tea bag – aware of the selfsame chinking rituals from next door.

The grander the hotel, the greater the potential for embarrassment. So as I approached the palatial Hotel Posh in Manchester on a Tuesday evening, my heart fluttered with foreboding. I'd been booked in there by a TV company for which I had written a series. I just hoped I wasn't going to end up with egg on my face. I'd had no experience until now of Room Service and Bellhops, except in Marx Brothers films.

The moment I arrived in the lobby my heart had plummetted at the sight of the Bellhops. They only wanted to be helpful – to carry my bag. All I had to do in return was smile gracefully and deftly convey a tip – something that always makes me cringe. I knew that I was clean out of small change – or what I had was in the bottom of my handbag, covered in chewing gum and grit. So I carried my own bag, smiling in a way that suggested, 'It's not that I don't want to tip you, it's just that I don't want to put you to all that trouble on my behalf.'

Once I was safely in my room, what I wanted most of

all was a snooze. I wasn't quite in the arms of Morpheus, though we were definitely eyeing each other up, when an imperious knock on the door catapulted me from under my quilt, like a mushroom leaving a pancake that has been hit with a mallet. Outside the door stood a maid.

'Good evening, Madam,' she smiled. 'Would you like me to turn down your bed?' For a moment I was tempted to say that the bed wasn't too loud at all: it was the door that was keeping me awake. The bed was fine, I insisted. I'd managed to turn it down all by myself.

Well, I had negotiated the first of those excruciating hotel encounters with strangers who wish to invade your bedroom and do things for you. I was doing quite well. I wasn't going to make a total ass of myself, as my Dad had done in Switzerland, back in the Fifties. Then I had drifted to sleep in my little bed in a corner of my parents' room.

In the dead of the night, my Dad was suddenly awoken by the need to go to the loo. He was leaning against the wall in the dark, putting his slippers on, when he unwittingly placed his hand upon the bell. Soon a breathless maid in her dressing gown knocked on the door and enquired in French what was wrong.

What my Dad said was 'C'est un accident,' meaning, 'I did it by accident.' 'Sey it ern axidong,' he murmured in that agony of effort which invariably accompanies British attempts to speak French. The maid misunderstood. An accident! She screamed. Had Madame perhaps fallen out of the bed? The window? Had someone suffocated beneath the duvet? Overdosed on Toblerone?

These memories of past humiliations seemed like ancient history to me, though, as I lounged in bed at the Hotel Posh the next morning, waiting for Room Service to bring me my Continental Breakfast. The only moment of uncertainty was when the maid brought the tray and I tried to indicate, by means of a scintillating smile, that I was not not tipping her because I was mean, but because I was too nice a person to bother with all that. I'm sure she understood.

Eventually I got up, showered, and put on my undies. Black bra and white pants actually – unfortunate, but at least it showed abhorrence for apartheid. Then I remembered that I was supposed to put the tray outside the door when I'd finished with it. I opened the door and peeped out: no one about. I bent down, placed the tray on the floor, and – Whump! The door swung to behind me, clouting me unceremoniously on the bottom and making me leapfrog over the tray and hit my head on the wall opposite. And then – Ker-Snap! The door was irrevocably locked, and I was shut out in a public corridor, wearing only undies *and they didn't even match!*

What should I do? Knock on an adjoining door? Or would that be misunderstood? Stride confidently down to the lobby in the manner of those wonderful old advertisements: *I dreamed I went shopping in my Maidenform bra?* What would Princess Anne do in a situation like this? Finally, I did what any sensible person would have done: I loitered, furtively, in an agony of shame.

Then, around the corner came – the maid! She realised in a split second the inconvenience of my situation, whipped out her keys, and had me back in my room in a trice without so much as a smirk. A £1 coin lay on the table: I pressed it wordlessly into her hand. I think I would've done the same had it been a £5 note. And even that would have been inadequate to express my true feelings at that moment. That's the trouble with tips: most of the time they're ludicrously unnecessary, but once in a blue moon they become totally inadequate.

I think I shall be staying at Hazeldene Guest House from now on. You have to get dressed for breakfast there. And it's nice to know that whatever embarrassing things happen to you in the dining room, you're unlikely ever to find yourself caught unawares in your underwear.

Insomnia

I can get all the way to the bathroom and back without even opening my eyes, in the middle of the night. Unfortunately I'd forgotten that, in a moment of distraction at bed time, I'd closed the loo seat and put my daughter's pink plastic hippo bubble-bath container on it. If you've ever sat on a hippo after midnight you'll know that it's not a soothing experience – especially if it's got its mouth open.

The night before a trip to London, you must get a good night's sleep. Otherwise you'll go dizzy on the Piccadilly Line or come over queer in Selfridges. London itself will seem sinister and threatening – the Natural History Museum can quickly become the Natural Hysteria Museum, and Harrods, Horrids. No, you simply can't face the metropolis without having had a decent night's rest.

That's what I told myself as I toddled upstairs at 10pm, clutching my hot-water bottle. I just hoped my daughter wasn't going to shatter my golden slumbers with one of her vampire shrieks two hours before dawn. I'm a single parent these days, and the worst thing about it is not being able to croak, 'Your turn!' in the middle of the night.

Before switching off the light, I glanced at a few pages of a plant catalogue. This was a big mistake. By the time I'd got my head down and my eyes shut, my mind was racing with horticultural speculation. Could I persuade the Duchess of Albany to weep over a wall? (The Duchess, by the way, is a distinguished clematis.) Would she prove compatible with Parkdirektor Riggers? (A famous rose, which always makes me think, somehow, of a swarthy mustachioed figure in jodhpurs flourishing a whip.)

Or should I avoid these exotics and stick to Cotoneaster? And how exactly did one pronounce Cotoneaster? By the time I'd worked out seven different ways of pronouncing Cotoneaster, three of them in Welsh, it was midnight. Doesn't time fly when you're enjoying yourself? This horticultural speculation had to stop. I'd obviously have to replace my bedside reading with something much less gripping than plant catalogues.

Then Parkdirektor Riggers was back, his moustache gleaming in the gloaming, and he invited the Duchess to admire his ornamental pear. The Duchess trembled. Could this be the start of something perennial? If only I were a writer of romances, all this could go straight on to a little bedside tape recorder and be grist to my mill. But as it was it was only grist to insomnia.

At 1am I decided that I was failing to fall asleep because I needed a last trip to the loo. I can get all the way to the bathroom and back without even opening my eyes, in the middle of the night. Unfortunately I'd forgotten that, in a moment of distraction at bed time, I'd closed the loo seat and put my daughter's pink plastic hippo bubble-bath container on it. If you've ever sat on a hippo after midnight you'll know that it's not a soothing experience – especially if it's got its mouth open. Gratefully, I sank back into bed, and, I hoped, into the arms of Morpheus. But the Editor of *Good Housekeeping* materialised instead.

She flashed her dark gypsy eyes and demanded to know how next month's piece was coming along. 'Oh, nearly finished,' I lied. Help! What could I write about next month? I ransacked my brain, but there was nothing there at all except a small piece of used bubble gum, wrapped in a bus ticket.

That was it! I'd write about junk food. Bubble gum. Pasta shaped like aliens. Walnut whips. Whoops! Parkdirektor Riggers was back, cracking his Walnut Whip.

At 3am I switched on the light and took two paracetamol. They weren't sleeping pills, but you never know: they might stun me a bit. Besides, if this went on I was sure to get a headache, and I might as well take the pills now to save time. I found an old bottle of Vitamin B pills in the bedside drawer and almost took one of them, too. But no. That word Vitamin ... wasn't that from the Latin *Vita*, meaning life? Maybe I should take vitamins in the morning. Resurrection pills.

It was 3.20am. I did what I always do when I'm absolutely desperate: I curled up on my left side, and stuck one thumb in my mouth and the other in my navel, just like when I was a child – sort of plugged in at both ends.

But this time it did not lead to sleep. It led to a Latin word.

Vita. What a lovely name for a girl, as in Vita Sackville-West, that writer and gardener who'd taken Virginia Woolf's fancy. And no wonder. Vita was tall, aristocratic, wore jodhpurs, . . . wait! Was Vita Sackville-West somehow both the Duchess of Albany and Parkdirektor Riggers?

This was it. I would write a romance. The love affair of the century, which led to the birth of an extraordinary woman: (better change the name slightly) Rita Sackcloth-Vest. Never mind sleep. I was wide awake now, in a white-hot furnace of frantic literary creativity.

'Mummy! Mummy!'

Jolted awake from a strange dream about Ryvita, I grabbed the clock. 5.30am. 'Want to come in your bed.' I attempted a croak of protest but my vocal chords, along with everything else, were paralysed with fatigue. My daughter crawled in behind me, and my kidneys cringed in unison in anticipation of her hard little feet. Bang! Thump! There they were.

At 6am we got up and had a bath. At 8.30am I took her to school, at just after nine I caught the London train, and at 11.45am precisely I came over queer in Selfridges.

But the really disappointing thing was that I realised that the great romance that led to Rita Sackcloth-Vest was a nonstarter. Though the next time I had insomnia, I got very taken with the idea of a sequel: Rita meets famous writer Virginia Fox, who travels to the Arctic and invents Glacier Mints. But I thought better of it in the morning.

Ghosts

All this was particularly disappointing because I have a psychic mother. She's one of those small Welsh women who are mysteriously in tune with the universe. She grew up in wild Montgomeryshire, you see, with the call of curlews in her ears. I grew up in Bletchley opposite the brickworks. I think Bletchley blighted my spiritual antennae, to be honest.

At times like this – Halloween, I mean – I become uneasily aware that I live in a very haunted part of the world: the West Country. We've got enough screaming skulls hereabouts to start a pop group. Brown ladies disappearing into the panelling? We're infested. And headless coachmen are two a penny – it's the only explanation for some of the terrible driving around here. But have I *seen* one? Well, actually . . . no.

I nearly saw a ghost once. I was staying in a house in Devon which John Wesley had once visited, centuries ago. And suddenly I was woken up in the middle of the night by the smell of Bibles. Terrifically strong, it was. Damp, old, mouldy Bibles. And guess what – when I woke up in the morning, the *pong was gone!* Oh all right, I admit I didn't actually *see* a ghost. But I definitely smelt one.

Our previous house was as near as you can get to Dracula's castle while still being suburban and semi-detached. It had strange gables that loomed out of the mist, and it was surrounded by gloomy, dripping evergreens. If ever I was going to see a ghost, it was here. Eagerly I inspected the mysterious damp patches on the carpet, only to find they were related to my daughter's potty training. Something like ectoplasm started oozing through the kitchen wall, but in the end we had to call in Rentokil, not the vicar.

It was all deeply frustrating. Here I was: credulous, eager, ready to break out into a cold sweat at a moment's notice, and where were they? I admit once I did hear faint groaning upstairs, and the sound of chains being dragged across the floor. But I found it was only Mrs Dibble, the cleaner, breathless from a life-and-death struggle with the Hoover.

It seemed I was destined to go through life unspooked. Admittedly I had felt strange on the garage roof at sunset when I was fifteen, but I think we can put that down to adolescence, don't you? I used to sit out at twilight, hoping for a Close Encounter of any kind at all, but the only spectral shape that ever materialised was my brother with a stocking mask over his face.

All this was particularly disappointing because I have a psychic mother. She's one of those small Welsh women who are mysteriously in tune with the universe. She grew up in wild Montgomeryshire, you see, with the call of curlews in her ears. I grew up in Bletchley opposite the brickworks. I think Bletchley blighted my spiritual antennae, to be honest.

Anyway, my mother knows what's going on even before it's started. She had an out-of-body experience when my brother was born. Come to think of it, he had an out-of-body experience, too. But hers was this archetypal here-I-am-floating-on-the-ceiling-looking-down-at-myself business. As she was hovering up there, she noticed the baby had a smudge of blood on his nose, from the forceps. And yet later, when she came round properly from the anaesthetic, his face was perfectly clean. But a nurse said there *had* been a smudge of blood but *they'd wiped it off while she was unconscious!*

Cripes! What do you think of that then? I tell you, it fair makes my spiritual antennae twang. Or would, if they hadn't been blighted by Bletchley.

Three years ago I moved out of Dracula's castle to share a nice modern house with my Mum and Dad. Well, I thought, that's it: if ever I was going to hear things that go bump in the night it was beneath those mist-shrouded gables. Nobody ever got goose pimples in a 1950s' semi, for goodness sake. *But that's just where I was wrong.*

A few months after we'd settled in, and were enjoying all that sensible modern design, my mother made a passing reference to the Black Shape. 'Oh,' I inquired, 'is that the latest PD James, she is brilliant isn't she?'

'Oh no,' said my mother casually, 'it's that thing that drifts up and down the hall, outside my bedroom.'

I went hot. I went cold. This was it! At last! A shape!

My mother revealed, upon interrogation, that though Black,

it was friendly, and sometimes even drifted past them while they were watching TV, and vanished into the bathroom. I was relieved to learn that, despite being supernatural, it was of a hygienic disposition.

Even my father had seen it disappearing around corners, and he had formed the impression that, though a Shape, it was also a woman. Well, we can't all be size ten.

I was really annoyed, though, that I myself repeatedly failed to catch even a glimpse of it. Even though I often have to tiptoe downstairs through my parents' quarters on my way to the kitchen for a glass of water, or aspirin.

Then one such night, arrayed as usual in my midnight-blue Marks & Sparks negligee, I fluttered past my parents' open door.

I heard my mother exclaim. 'There it goes, Dad!' she cried. 'Did you see it?' And then it dawned on me: the Black Shape was none other than yours truly.

For a while I was deeply disappointed. Then I had a thought that cheered me up a lot. After I'd kicked the bucket I'd actually be able to disappear into the wall, or cause interference on the TV. But then I realised how things will really be, given my luck. I'll haunt away till I'm blue in the face and no one will take a blind bit of notice.

Susceptibility to tears

I have a very trashy sensibility. I've sat dry-eyed through Beethoven's *Ode To Joy*, but show me a soup advert of man, boy and dog splashing through the rain towards a steaming cauldron of minestrone, and I'm howling.

I've got this problem. It started when I was about three years old. I was sucking my thumb at the time, and my mother was singing to me, as recommended by Dr Ezekial Shrubsole's *The Sacred Role Of Motherhood*.

'All the birds of the air were a-sighing and a-sobbing,' she sang – quite tunefully, being Welsh – 'when they heard of the death of poor Cock Robin . . .'

My little face crumpled up. My lower lip wobbled, my nose filled with saline solution. I took the thumb out of my mouth, threw my head back and Waaaaaaaaaa! I was away.

Ever since, I've been susceptible to tears. It's not just tragedies like the Death of Cock Robin that provoke them. I cry at comedies, too, since they show man's fragile attempts to make the best of fate's unyielding sombreness. Or something. I cry all the year round, undeterred by hosepipe bans, but I cry in a particularly Old-Trafford kind of way at Christmas, when there is so much to cry about. Cock Robins for a start, not dead, but no less tear-jerking alive and well, in pert little red-and-white woolly hats.

The more naff the Christmas card, the more readily my tear ducts seem to spring into action. But then, I have a very trashy sensibility. I've sat dry-eyed through Beethoven's *Ode To Joy*, but show me a soup advert of man, boy and dog splashing through the rain towards a steaming cauldron of minestrone, and I'm howling.

Yes, Christmas offers particularly tender traps to the unsuspecting eyeball. There's all that stuff about it being For The Children, and then the ordeal of Children In Hospital, Children Starving In Africa . . .

Last year, I determinedly plugged my ears against the word *children*. I was also determined not to flinch at any mention of snow, frost, bells, blazing logs, or robins. Having prepared my ears, I addressed my tear ducts – with gruff military determination. 'All right now, you chaps. I don't want any nonsense from you. Remember, there are no depths to which the wily tear-jerker will not stoop. Bung up your ducts with British grit, stiffen the upper lip, summon up the will, and affirm in the face of the foe: "We shall not be moved!" ' It was quite heroic really. Shakespearean. In the film, the role of my right tear duct will be played by Kenneth Branagh.

So, on Christmas morning, I emerged from the bedroom with a stoic dignity. I bore unflinchingly the sight of my daughter unpacking her stocking, though it was a poignant sight, reminding me of a hyena disembowelling a poor defenceless wildebeest. Dry-eyed, I watched endless video reruns of scrubbed choristers intoning '*Wonsin Rrroyal Defitz Asssittiee stowd a lowwwlyee cattaille shedde.*'

Even the Queen left me unmoved – and I've cried at every single one of the Queen's Christmas messages except the one with the barbecue. And I bet I'd have cried at that one too, if there'd been any sign at all of bowls of steaming soup.

But last year, my bearing was quite exemplary. I got through until nightfall without so much as a tremor, and I was feeling pretty pleased with myself, I can tell you. I was confident that I wasn't going to dissolve into tears, even if snow started to fall, and my daughter suddenly acquired a limp, a cough, and a saintly, radiant smile, instead of the scowl of exhausted greed which adorned her features by 8pm. I even managed to get past the Care Bears toothpaste tube totally unscathed: what more can be said?

But then, in a moment of carelessness, after my daughter had fallen asleep, I decided to clean the lavatory. It's one of those little rituals, you know. I do it every Christmas. I seized the bottle of ECOVER ecologically sound, fully biodegradable loo cleaner and – I was lost. On the front was a picture of a landscape, with a bird flying over a lake. NOT TESTED ON ANIMALS, it proclaimed. A little snivel escaped me at the thought of all the dear animals with friendly eyes that the Ecover people weren't testing on.

FOR PEOPLE WHO CARE ABOUT THE ENVIRONMENT, it went on. Suddenly they were all there in my imagination: those sweet, idealistic souls, trudging home from the Hampstead Health Store with their Traidcraft basket full of fly killer that wouldn't hurt a fly: it just persuades them to leave. Friends of the Earth! My eyes brimmed at the thought.

DOES NOT AFFECT SEPTIC TANKS, it said. Darling old septic tanks! Snug and uncomplaining under their cosy lawns, faithfully going about their business, and doing things for us that even our best friends would baulk at. Tears burst from my eyes, as, hopelessly caught up in the thoroughly inspiring drama of it all, I continued to read on with trepidation.

SQUIRT A SMALL AMOUNT UNDER THE RIM . . . AND LEAVE IT OVERNIGHT TO ALLOW ITS GENTLE ACTION TO WORK. Oh dear! . . . *Gentle!* Now there's a word that can provoke a half-pint of tears, on a wobbly premenstrual evening, without any help from a single noun.

But 'Heads down, men!' I cried, 'Here come the nouns.' THE PINE, CITRUS, LAVENDER, CITRONELLA AND EUCALYPTUS OILS ACT AS A MILD DISINFECTANT. And all of a sudden, there I was, magically transported to an atmospheric Mediterranean wood. The most beautiful aromatic trees in the world were breathing all around me in the heat. Summer! Beautiful, warm, glorious, scented summer! Oh how I missed it! How I longed for it! That unsurpassed gift from the gods to humanity! Waaah!

Mere recycled loo paper wasn't going to be equal to this flow of tears. I seized the nearest bath towel, sat down on the edge of the bath, and then I let rip.

If you can't beat it, give in to it. I think there's a strong possibility I'll be spending next Christmas at Disneyland.

Fax machines

Filofaxes are tiresomely thick and self-important diary thingies in which you lose information that could more efficiently be stored on the back of an old envelope in the teapot on the mantelpiece.

Come on, I told myself, it's a new year, a nearly-new decade: we simply must get to grips with the technology of the future. And here, decorated with a tinsel bow and a sprig of holly, was this lovely new Fax machine all ready to do . . . whatever it is Faxes do. I had the *User's Guide*. But what I really needed was the nursery guide to Fax machines. Something like 'Once upon a time there were three little Faxes . . .'

I used to think Fax was just an unpretentious sort of FiloFax. Mind you, I used to think Filofax was a character in Shakespeare: along with Falstaff, Philostrate and Sycorax. But no! As everyone knows by now, Filofaxes are tiresomely thick and self-important diary thingies in which you lose information that could more efficiently be stored on the back of an old envelope in the teapot on the mantelpiece.

But Faxes . . . now they're really clever. Fax is nothing to do with facts; it's short for facsimile, which is a snooty word for Copy, especially the sort of copy that's exactly like the original. (As the Oxford Professor of History proudly remarked of his eldest daughter, 'She's an absolute facsimile of her mother.')

If you want to send someone a letter, you feed it into your machine, dial the Fax number of the place you want to send it to, and lo! The sheet of paper goes chugging through your machine, out the other side, and somehow all the words on it get read, understood and sent off down the telephone line to emerge on to a blank piece of paper in the receiving machine at the other end.

Staggering, isn't it? What I wanted to know was, how do I do it? The only way I could imagine words going down wires was in sticks of seaside rock. The man who'd delivered it couldn't enlighten me. 'I just happened to be going down the A46 so they told me to drop it off,' he said, backing defensively towards the door. 'They're dead simple. Give Paul a ring.'

Paul was the man on the end of the phone who had supplied the Fax machine, you see. His manner was, well, halfway between brisk and brusque. Sort of briusque.

'They're extremely simple machines,' he said, when I rang him to ask if he could possibly come over and get mine going. 'It's all in the manual. But if you get stuck, call back.'

I got stuck in. I got it all wired up, with a bit of help from my Dad. I studied the KEYS AND THEIR USES section of the manual, though I felt a twinge of seasickness when I came to the KEYPAD (alphanumeric) one. But I felt optimistic. Perhaps I wasn't going to be foxed by my Fax at all. I'd soon get the hang of the ins and outs of it. Document In Tray said the helpful diagram, pointing to the front: Document Out Tray, pointing to the back. Well, that seemed straightforward. Obviously when documents came in, they'd arrive at the front, and when you wanted to send something out, you loaded it at the back.

I rang up my agent and asked her to send me a Fax. Breathlessly I waited for it to come through. Suddenly the machine gave a tiny, urgent newborn yelp, and a piece of paper came miraculously chugging out of the front.

'You clever little thing!' I cried, patting its keypad. All I had to do now was to send something out. I put the document ready in the Document Out Tray, dialled the number, and pressed START. Nothing happened. A message flashed up. RECEIVE, it said. 'No darling, not Receive, Send!' I coaxed, RECEIVE, it insisted. 'Now don't be naughty, just do as mummy says.' 'RECEIVE.' I lost my temper and gave it a smart little tap across the keys. It emitted a piercing cry of pain. I hoped there were no snoopers hanging about outside from the Anti-Faxhurting Brigade. For half an hour I tried to tempt it, I even put a little bit of sugar on the end of the paper. But it just sulked.

'All right!' I snapped, 'I'm telling your father!' And I rang up Paul. He listened patiently.

'You just feed the document in,' he said, 'and it grabs it.'

'But it doesn't grab it!' I wailed. 'It won't even touch it! It's just not interested.'

Paul made soothing noises and said he would get Peter to ring me. I was certainly getting my share of Apostolic Attention. Maybe if Peter was stumped I'd get a call from the Almighty Himself, maybe a Fax. God'll fix it, I thought, on my knees. After all, he moves in a mysterious way . . .

Waiting for my call, I stared in desperation at my unco-operative little machine. It wouldn't eat! And if it wouldn't eat, how could it thrive? I was a failure as a Fax operator. I burst into tears. Then Peter rang. He was more cheerful than Paul, just like in the Bible.

'Right,' he said. 'Put the document in at the front.'

'At the front?' I gasped.

All was made clear. I blushed, I stammered, I wished the floor would swallow me up. I'd been trying to shove the document in at the wrong end. If you tried the same thing with a baby's bottle I don't suppose the baby would be very cooperative, either.

The lure of the small ads in *Old Moore's Almanack*

In the deep midwinter, there's nothing I like more than crouching by candlelight over a copy of *Old Moore's Almanack* and seeing what the New Year has in store: for me personally, for the nation, for the world. Being a nosy type, I started off with horoscopes of the famous. Prince Charles, for example, should be warned that beyond 1991 Saturn will enter his Aquarian seventh house. Well, I suppose if you have so many houses, it must be a full-time job keeping an eye on them all.

Then I got stuck into what the future holds now that Mrs Thatcher has left number ten – I was halfway through the more-than-welcome news that *unbridled capitalism would come under scrutiny as a destructive force* when something caught my eye. It was a small advert.

'Secrets of Finger Magic,' it read. 'Finger magic requires no long rituals or equipment, and can even be used by one in a crowded room or bus.' It didn't say whether finger magic could get you released from custody afterwards, though.

What it did promise, however, was dramatic. 'Settlement of debts! . . . Fulfilment of sexual desire! . . . End of insomnia! . . . Make a neighbour move away! . . . Control children!' . . . Hang on a minute! Was that *control children*? With a mere finger? Now that really does sound like magic. I'm completely unable to control children even when brandishing a Mason Pearson hairbrush of the bristliest kind while yelling blue murder.

Turning tactfully away from the question of sexual fulfilment through finger magic, I considered the much more pressing problem of my debt to Access. Would they, in lieu of the £999 I owed them, accept a gesture from my magic finger? I was doubtful. And I was even more sceptical about getting unpleasant neighbours to move away. I did have some, once, when I lived in Cambridge, but I'm sure if I'd dared to poke a magic finger through their letter box, they'd have bitten it off.

I was in two minds about finger magic. But the next ad really got to the heart of things: 'How To Look Incredibly Young/How To Become Taller.' It promised 'Potent Mind Techniques for looking much younger, also a unique exercise for becoming taller.' Actually, I've already got an unique exercise for becoming taller. It's bending down and putting on my old 1970s' high heels. Now they're really magic. Not only do they make me look at least six inches taller but also magically anguished.

I decided to postpone looking incredibly young until I felt up to it. Maybe another twenty years. Also, if their Mind Technique was all that Potent, I thought I might as well present it with a real challenge. I turned the page, eager for more life-transforming advertisements.

And what did I find? 'Rub the Buddha for Money.' What a brilliant concept. So much more fun than queuing up for hours at the cashpoint and then getting that rude Refer To Bank message, with everyone else in the queue smirking in a superior way. I was urged to send off that very second for my own Buddha, at the bargain price of £10, which would be rushed to me posthaste. Then whenever I was a bit short of the ready, all I would have to do was 'Take the Buddha in your right hand and gently rub his magic belly. It's that simple!' It had a money-back guarantee, as it were. It didn't say, though, if you could double your money if you rubbed the Buddha's belly with your magic finger.

And Buddha was not the only transcendent figure from world religion to appear rather unexpectedly in *Old Moore's Almanack*. 'Jesus Christ – the truth at last!' screamed another ad. 'What the Gospels *don't* tell you – the Amazing Truth about Jesus and Satan!' No, don't tell me, I can guess: they're running a hamburger restaurant together in downtown San Francisco.

Never before have I encountered so many promises to change my life for a tenner. I couldn't face the '365 Ways

To Have A Happy Sex Life' nor 'Spot The Ball – How To Win.' (I should add that these two ads were entirely unconnected, by the way.) I resisted – just – the impulse to send away for a magic cream which would give me a 'Full Round Eye-Catching Bust in six weeks,' mainly because it didn't say whose. Also I've managed perfectly well without one for the past twenty-five years. And anyway, I certainly didn't want anything to get in the way of my magic finger.

I hesitated, but not fatally, over the Lucky Oak Leaf for only £2, before recalling that there was a three-foot high pile of free ones rotting out in the garden. I found myself at a loss for words when faced with the challenging question, 'Why Are You A Bore?' even though I recognised all too clearly the justice of its accusation.

But what I couldn't resist even for a moment was another somewhat optimistic promise: Astral Projection. 'How To Travel Anywhere Outside Your Body.' Now this was what I'd always wanted. The perfect hassle-free holiday! Mexico without the tummy bugs! St Kitts without the sunburn! A Mediterranean cruise without seasickness! No more getting stranded at airports, no more suitcases full of dirty laundry, no more crawling along the M25!

Could I start with a weekend in Prague? And then a fortnight in the Seychelles? . . . Did the travel agents know about this? And – most important – could I do next year's Christmas shopping by Astral Projection? After all, I'm still nursing the bruises from last year's.

All in all, I'm really very hopeful about the possibilities of Astral Projection. Watch this space.

The *Question Time* lunch and the right to silence

Political arguments are particularly difficult, because I can all too easily see the opposing point of view. I've even, when watching *Question Time*, found myself agreeing with Norman Tebbit.

It was in the spring of 1989 that I failed the scalding soup test. I've cringed privately at the memory of it, but perhaps the best way to exorcise it is to tell you the full grisly tale. It also provides the answer to the burning question: why have I never appeared on BBC TV's *Question Time*? That late-night programme of Political Debate, which used to be chaired by the cheerily scowling Sir Robin Day, and is now presented by the sexy but unsmiling Mr Peter Sissons. Two years ago, the European Elections loomed and I was a Green Party candidate. So when the producer of *Question Time* rang up, I should have been thrilled. It was my chance to Speak Out.

But what I actually did, right after the phone call, was to run upstairs and hide my head under the pillow. This was not, you understand, panic at the thought of appearing on *Question Time*. I had so far only been invited to The Lunch.

You can imagine how embarrassing it would be if, when Peter Sissons asked, 'And what's the Green Party's line on this?' The Green Party's answer was 'Er . . . er . . . help! I think I'm going to faint.' So, in order to weed out the weeds, regular lunches were held where the people running the programme – a fiercely intelligent pair of women – scrutinised their victims for signs of mumbling or fainting.

There were four of us on trial: a tall, dashing, assertive theological bod, a tall, dashing, assertive business bod, a distinguished diplomat who had the tact not to be tall or assertive, and me. The Muslim diplomat preserved a digni-fied silence as the air crackled with the dynamic wit of the two assertive bods and the fierce women.

I tried to pretend that I was saying nothing because I was dignified and distinguished like the Muslim diplomat. But actually, it was because it was a full-time job dealing with the soup. It was scalding hot and had long strands of carrot floating in it, like seaweed in the Sargasso Sea. It was a choice between choking and a severely burnt tongue.

Suddenly, the business bod pounced on me. It was a cruel moment to choose, as I had strands of scalding carrot dangling all down my chin, rather like the ginger beard of opposition health spokesman Robin Cook.

'What's the Green Party going to do for *me*?' demanded the business bod. Alas, though I had Robin Cook's beard, I lacked his eloquence.

'Er ... er ...' I mumbled, and was instantly interrupted by the theological bod.

In bed that night, I realised that what I should have said was: 'Ask not what the Green Party can do for you, ask what you can do for er, er, the world, the environment the, the planet-type thingy.' But this brilliant gem of self-expression came to me too late.

At the time, all I could feel was gratitude to the theological bod for interrupting me so early on in my struggle. I was even more grateful to the Muslim diplomat, as he had not said anything at all so far – not even er, er. Perhaps he'd burnt his tongue too. Mine was so sore, business would've sounded like bithnith and Sissons, Thithonth.

One of the fierce women decided it was time to draw the Muslim diplomat out, and asked him about that other burning issue: *The Thatanic Vertheth* by Thalman Ruthdie. With dignity and at great length, he explained the offence that had been caused by the book in the Muslim world. At this we all fell silent. My gratitude to the Muslim diplomat increased. The more of us who were silent, the less obvious would my own silence be. Eventually one of the assertive bods said Yes, we do understand, we do regret the offence caused, but after all it's Free Speech, you know. Whereupon the Muslim diplomat went into extraordinary detail for a few hours about the Koran.

Yes, said one of the fierce women, what seemed like several days later, we do sympathise, but after all, you know, Free Speech, et cetera. Whereupon the Muslim diplomat amplified his original statement for another very long time: until the blue, coconut ice cream arrived, in fact. I was desperate for ice to soothe my scalded tongue, but somehow the blueness of it proved a huge obstacle. I'd never eaten anything blue except a Smartie before, and I was too old to attempt such an unnatural act in public.

A few more pathetic attempts were made to raise a cheer for Free Speech, but I was not convinced. I'd had just about as much as I could take of Free Speech. It was Free Speech that had got me into this mess in the first place.

It was perhaps at that moment that I realised I wasn't a politician at heart. It wasn't that I didn't believe in the Green cause. I am, as you'll know from the blurb alongside this column, an ardent conservationist. But I'm not an ardent conversationist.

Ordinary speaking is enough of an ordeal for me: arguments, particularly political arguments, are somehow impossible. This may be because my family never had arguments, so I never learnt to argue as a child, or to distinguish between the healthy, enjoyable argument, and the full-blown, bitter, vindictive, saucepan-hurling row.

Political arguments are particularly difficult, because I can all too easily see the opposing point of view. I've even, when watching *Question Time*, found myself agreeing with Norman Tebbit.

Of course I'm in favour of Free Speech. I would defend to my dying breath the right of Norman Tebbit to have opinions and of Mr Thithonth to tease them out of him. But I would defend even more urgently my right to silence.

Mind you, I was a little disappointed that I never got asked to appear on *Question Time*. After the ordeal of The Lunch, the programme itself would have been a pushover.

Awards ceremony

I was introduced to Prince
Charles once when we were
both undergraduates and my
hand managed somehow to
miss his hand altogether and
go whizzing on up inside
his sleeve towards the Royal
armpit.

Excuse me if I sound a little exhausted today. I'm thinking of changing my name to Limp. The reason is I've just sat through my first Awards Ceremony. You know the sort of occasion I mean: it's got glitter, it's got glitz; The London Palladium is packed to the gunwales with celebs, and a Major Artiste officiates as Master or Mistress of Ceremonies.

Writers, Directors, Actors and Actresses, etc, are nominated for awards in various categories. Most Promising Newcomer, Best Character Actress, Best Pedigree Ram . . . (Warren Beatty usually wins that one). No, wait, I'm getting muddled up with the Smithfield Show. And that would never do, because Imelda is a vegetarian.

Imelda Staunton was the reason I was there, you see. She played Izzy in the Granada ITV series, *Up The Garden Path*, which I wrote. Imelda had been nominated for Most Promising Newcomer, but if she won she wouldn't be able to accept it in person as she was appearing in a West-End Show.

'So,' said producer Humphrey Barclay, 'we thought it would be rather nice if you could accept it for her.'

Imelda deserves every accolade going, I reckon. But my fingernails melted with fear at the possibility of having to go up on the stage of The Palladium under the glare of TV lights and shake hands with a Major Artiste. I'm rather bad at that sort of thing. I was introduced to Prince Charles once when we were both undergraduates and my hand managed somehow to miss his hand altogether and go whizzing on up inside his sleeve towards the Royal armpit.

As for the dreaded speech, I started trying to draft it the

minute Humphrey rang and wrestled with it for the whole of the next fortnight until the Awards Day finally dawned. I knew that if she won, Imelda would want to thank, above all, Humphrey Barclay and Jonathan James-Moore, who had cast her in the original Radio 4 series.

'Imelda would like to thank Humphathon Bark-Moore and Jonathrey Jameclay – I mean, Humphclay Barcphrey – er.' Cripes. Suddenly it seemed that everybody had an anagram or an Aztec incantation instead of a name.

I had to get the producers' names right, though. I'd go through it in my head just one more time. 'Ladies and Gents –' Wait! What if there were Lords and Kings? Hordes of the things? After all, show business is full of aristocrats: Duke Ellington, The Marquis of Granby . . . or is he a pub? And what does one call Jimmy Savile these days? Lord Jim?

As for Royalty, well, my toenails turned to ice. Just what degree of grovelling might be necessary? And given that I'd crammed myself into a size ten little black dress held together with old nappy pins, just how much grovelling could I contemplate without a fatal ripping sound?

And what about Dames? The place could be full of them. Dame Edna Everage, Dame Kiri Te Kanawa. How did you address them? What was their male equivalent? I tried in vain to think of it, but the nearest I got was Guys and Dolls. I shuddered in my seat in the stalls, mentally still rehearsing even though the show was already well under way. 'Your Majesty, Your Royal Highnesses, Prince Harry, My Lords, Earls, Dukes, Knights and Days, Guys 'n' Dolls, Amos 'n' Andy, Dame Kiri Te Kanawa, Madonna, Mammy! Mummee! I want my Mummeeeee!'

But this was madness. All I had to do – if Imelda won – was say 'Thanks very much from Imelda!' and run like hell.

Her category was coming up now: they were showing clips of the three short-listed nominees. Suddenly a huddle of cameramen came stampeding up our aisle and stopped at the end of our row. I've always wondered whether the people who are going to win are in the know. Well, one thing's certain: the cameramen certainly are.

I thought I'd better start blushing. I hate leaving things till the last minute. So even before the name came out of the envelope, my spit had all dried up, my bones had turned to latex, and my heart was bouncing around like a demented sumo wrestler on a pogo stick. And then . . . in unison, the cameramen turned their backs on our row and started dazzling away at a different block of seats, across the aisle. The awful truth dawned on me: someone else had won.

I went through the motions of clapping and everything, but my entire body was in chaos. It had produced enough adrenalin to get me up on to the stage of The London Palladium – about six gallons, I should think. And now I didn't have to make that terrifying journey, I was stuck with all that adrenalin. It sloshed about in my muscles, urging me to do all sorts of rash things.

It wanted me to get up, shout 'Shame!' rip up my seat, hurl it at the stage, leap over the heads of my neighbours and into the aisle, cry: 'God for England, Harry and St Imelda!' and, wresting the trophy from the winner's hands, soar upwards with it on a pillar of fire, burst triumphantly through the roof of The Palladium, and flash westwards with it across the night sky to Imelda's flat in Paddington.

You know adrenalin. It always thinks big. I didn't take any notice of its suggestions, of course. I knew if I just sat still it would eventually turn quietly back into cellulite, or something. And though not winning the award might mean a split second of disappointment for Imelda, it would be a lifetime of relief for me.

Travelling by train with a child

She started to jiggle about rhythmically on my knee. I whispered an urgent inquiry: was it necessary to visit the loo? No, she replied sternly, the music was making her dance sitting down. I was still smiling at this rather charming remark, when she started singing along with the inaudible tape: 'I'm just a sweet Trans . . . vestite from Transsexual . . . Transylvania . . . ia!' she bawled.

'I think we'll go there by train, darling, won't that be marvellous?' My daughter's face lit up with a kind of brightness only previously provoked by Salt & Vinegar Crisps. Going by train was a treat.

It was secretly my treat, in fact. Driving the car from Gloucestershire to Norfolk would mean at least an hour on the M25, wouldn't it? An hour on the M25! I'd rather have six hours with MI5.

Of course one could avoid London altogether and strike out daringly across country. But I had a suspicion that if I tried it, I'd get irrevocably tangled up in Milton Keynes. My expensive education had warned me to stay well clear of Milton and Keynes, let alone both at once. So we went by train.

We were heading, incidentally, for Center Parcs: a holiday 'village' with pools, water chutes, palms and Jacuzzis, all under a big glass dome. A fragment of tropical paradise not far from Thetford. It sounds unlikely. But it's just the place, in chilly April, to take a child who wants to be a mermaid.

We caught the train, bagged a table, and instantly buried it beneath the colouring book, the drawing book, the felt-tip pens, the Lego and the jigsaw puzzle of Jeremy Fisher.

'Swindonthis sis Swindon Swind donthi sis Swindon,' boomed a station announcement twenty minutes later.

'Are we still in England?' whispered my child.

A squall of rain hit the window at the very moment I realised we had to change at Swindon. I leapt up, swept the drawing book, the colouring book, and Jeremy Fisher into a bag. Felt-tip pens flew everywhere, a puce one lodging, unperceived, in the tweed folds of a countrywoman's skirt. I left it where it was. If that countrywoman was you, Madam, do send me the dry-cleaning bill.

There's nothing like hauling two heavy suitcases, a rucksack and a small, short-sighted child out of a train and into the rain at Swindon, to make you realise that – for single parents at least – train travel might not be such a treat after all. Where, oh where, has he gone? Not the husband – the British Rail porter. He has vanished from his natural habitat without the World Wide Fund For Nature raising a murmur. As mysterious as the demise of the dinosaurs, but infinitely more inconvenient.

We got on the London train only to find most of the Welsh nation snugly ensconced, apparently all doing their bit for rural depopulation at once. I spied one free single seat.

'You can sit on Mummy's knee, darling,' I whispered. 'And listen to Roald Dahl on your Walkman.'

'Snot Roald Dahl!' retorted my dear child in that unnecessarily loud voice often used by people trapped by Walkmen or hairdriers. 'Smusic!'

'Very nice, dear,' I murmured. 'No need to shout.' She started to jiggle about rhythmically on my knee. I whispered an urgent inquiry. Was it necessary to visit the loo? No, she replied sternly, the music was making her dance sitting down. I was still smiling at this rather charming remark, when she started singing along with the inaudible tape: 'I'm just a sweet Trans . . . vestite from Transsexual . . . Transylvania . . . ia!' she bawled.

'What the –' I seized the Walkman and Ejected. Tape from machine, I mean, not us from train. That refinement is not yet available, alas. Somehow Roald Dahl had been replaced by my old cassette of The Rocky Horror Show. 'We mustn't disturb other people, darling. Why not do some of your lovely drawings?' Children often accompany their drawings with dialogue – but rather too loudly in her case. 'Cinderella married the Prince,' she intoned, 'and he gave her the seeds for five babies and this is a drawing of him giving her the seeds.'

The eyes of our Welsh fellow travellers instantly swivelled towards her drawing book. I was temporarily blinded by a vast blush, but when my vision cleared, I was relieved to find His Royal Highness solemnly handing Cinderella a tasteful packet – Sutton's F1 Hybrids, evidently.

'Paddington!' I exclaimed in relief.

'Where?' cried my child. 'And has he got his hat on?'

This moment was almost as disappointing to her as the revelation, a couple of years ago, that the Green Party did not have balloons and a conjurer.

Anyone rash enough to try to cross London by Tube with a small child and suitcases deserves a medal – or a medical certificate. My daughter was so charmed by the escalators that she begged to go up and down them again. I retorted that the very thought of it made me want to scream.

By the time we reached Liverpool Street Station, I was hallucinating, and hoping for a nonstop express train to Thetford, with an in-car toy shop selling Sindy dolls at 5p each and a British Rail cinema showing ET. We found ourselves instead on the 3.45 to Cambridge, which stops not only at every single station, but at every interesting field – sometimes, it seemed, at every blade of grass.

It stopped at Great Shelford. It stopped at Little Shelford. It stopped at Middle-Sized Shelford. It stopped at Over-Forty-and-Still-on-the-Shelford.

'How many more stops?' whined my daughter, hurling the hapless Jeremy Fisher to the floor.

I dared not tell her fifteen. So I suggested that we play I-Spy and informed her I spied something beginning with C.

'Cockup,' she suggested, without a moment's hesitation. Out of the mouths of babes . . .

Center Parcs, by the way, was well worth the ordeal. And best of all, while we were there we bumped into an old Welsh friend, who gave us a lift home in his quiet, private Volvo. But boy, did we get tangled up in Milton Keynes.

Jigsaws

Once a year I allow myself a really futile experience: The Jigsaw. It's my mother's fault. She leads me astray. She orders these fiendish jigsaws from the charity catalogues – huge, two thousand-piece affairs.

Last year it was the Royal Family. We spent hours loyally scrabbling through fragments of tiara for the Princess of Wales's glittering smile. And I well remember one dim twilight session when Prince Philip's boot was found mysteriously embedded in Prince Edward's backside.

Luckily, this year's jigsaw was not so controversial. It was a sylvan scene: an enchanting little cottage set in acres of rolling British countryside, the only occupants of wood and meadow being a selection of British birds. It was the kind of jigsaw you felt you wanted to spend a weekend in. Now, with jigsaws, a weekend can turn overnight into three hundred years. But I braced myself. I needed it.

I'm a bit shaky on my British birds, especially for someone who's been described for some time alongside this column as an avid conservationist. To be honest, I don't know my Bluetits from my Spotted Redshanks. And apart from its educational value, of course, the jigsaw was going to supply rest and relaxation, peace and quiet, and bring to my tired soul the balm of contemplation.

I removed the breadcrumbs and dog hairs from the table, while my mother turned the jigsaw out of its box and sorted it into piles: a huge pile of sky, a massive pile of green stuff, and a small heap of bits of birds. She also found and skilfully assembled the edges. Every jigsawyer knows that you must start on the outside, or things can go disastrously wrong, as with a soft-boiled egg.

A day later we'd achieved two square inches of sky. I felt a bit ashamed. After all, God created the world in six days.

Astronomers debate about whether the world was created with a big bang, but I incline to the cosmic jigsaw-puzzle theory. There are so obviously pieces missing, after all. A decent design for the sardine tin, for example. But I suppose that's man's negligence, not God's.

On the second day I knocked off the sweet little cottage in no time, as it consisted of nice straight bricks and tiles. The great thing about tiles is you can instantly see which way up they're supposed to be. Although a chap once came to mend the roof who obviously hadn't done enough jigsaws. But my success with the cottage cheered me up. 'I can feel this doing me good,' I remarked to my mother, flexing my fingers boastfully. A rash observation, and one which often leads to a major fracture. But my mother did not reply. She was still wrestling with the sky, and no doubt wishing there were more clouds in it. Why this awful, pure, bright blue? Why was there not a light aircraft pulling a banner reading 'Happy Anniversary Stan And Gertie' or 'Archie Dean For Troublefree Ironmongery'?

Once we'd assembled the birds – a mere week's work, with hardly a mishap unless you count putting the robin's leg on upside down – I realised with a sinking feeling that we were now condemned to the pastoral idyll. Three million pieces of leaf and grass awaited us. There was ivy, there was periwinkle, there was oak, there was cherry, and I was blowed if I could tell the difference between them.

It was at this moment that I realised the great mistake of creation. *All the leaves don't hang downwards.* They cheerfully toss and dance, don't they, all anyhow? Now although this might be delightful in the sight of the Lord, the rambler, the landscape painter and other such romantic blokes, to us dedicated jigsawyers it's darned inconvenient. It means that every piece of leaf has to be rotated through 360, or possibly 990, degrees before it can be discarded with a deep groan.

Time passed. The contents of the fridge turned silently to coal. My father learned to cook in self-defence. My six-year-old daughter stripped down to her leotard and went off to live with the dog at the bottom of the garden. It was a load off my mind, knowing that she was well cared for.

My mother and I were still locked in mortal combat with the leaves. At times, I admit, my Green principles trembled and I fantasised about herbicide. What use was all this green emptiness? Oh, that the planners had been let loose on it! It seemed such a waste not to have a motorway running slap through the middle, a housing estate on one side and a nice garish video-hire place on the other.

Finally, however, my mother snapped the last oak leaf satisfyingly on to its twig, and I slumped insensible on to the carpet. I heard her footsteps echo down the hall. I knew where she was going. To fetch the camera and put the kettle on. There was nothing I needed more than a cup of tea. As long as it wasn't Green.

The jigsaw was duly photographed and then allowed to lie in state for several days so that the respectful crowds could file past and sign the Book of Admiration. But eventually, not without a sense of anguished vandalism, it was swept away into its box. But the scars upon my soul remain. I have decided in all conscience I cannot continue to describe myself as an avid conservationist, so we've changed the blurb at the side of this column.

My mother, however, has emerged from the experience with new and frightening purpose. Even now she's scanning this season's Mencap catalogue. And, judging by the glint in her eye, I think she's settled on the one on page twenty-three – a jigsaw of a giant snooker table. Without the balls.

Breaking wine glasses

One of Wendy's beautiful glasses leapt from my wet hands, performed a brief pas de deux with the cold tap, and smashed to bits.

I don't know why it is, but I'm always running out of wineglasses. No, wait, I do know why it is. It's because when I'm washing up, wineglasses seem to say to themselves, 'I want to be a dancer!', pirouette wildly out of my fingers and crash to their deaths on the draining board. It has its benefits, of course. In our house we've already realised John Major's ideal of a glassless society.

But it can also be disastrous. I realised this last Saturday at 5.32pm – two minutes after all the shops had irrevocably shut. That evening I was entertaining five charming friends. It was to be quite an elegant evening, by my standards. I was going to make a real effort to transcend my usual abysmally dull culinary performance. We were to dine on Toad In The Hole De Gaulle and Spotted Dick A La Plume De Ma Tante. I'd scraped most of the Play-Doh off the lino; the Toad and Spotted Dick were coming along nicely; a few bottles of Beaujolais were warming under the tea cosy. *But what were we going to drink them out of?* It threw me into such a panic, I thought in italics and ended with a preposition – something writers try not to do even when alone.

I assembled a motley collection of vessels; one wine glass (cracked); one pint glass (stolen in an excess of youthful bravado from The Frog and Nightgown in 1973, though what exactly Frogs could have to do with Nightgowns I shudder to think); one chipped Pooh Bear mug; one pre-War enamel tooth mug complete with mysterious stains; one hideous mock-pewter tankard with a glass bottom; one Tommee Tippee . . . This really would never do. It's a well-known fact that men don't make passes at girls who don't have proper glasses.

So I ran next door and borrowed a set of six beautiful, rather unusual glasses from my well-endowed and generous neighbour Wendy.

The dinner was OK: Toad and Dick disappeared without complaint, Beaujolais was quaffed (elegantly thanks to Wendy) by those not driving home, and all in all, washing up at midnight with my melodramatic friend Miranda, I reckoned it had been a success. Then it happened.

One of Wendy's beautiful glasses leapt from my wet hands, performed a brief pas de deux with the cold tap, and smashed to bits.

'Oh no!' cried Melodramatic Miranda. 'I'm sure I remember Wendy telling me those glasses were of great sentimental value!' A shadow fell across my soul.

Next morning I left my child in the care of her grandparents, with a choice of seventeen different toys to break before my return (she takes after me – it's quite charming). I leapt aboard the 8.05am to Paddington – not too recklessly, as I was clutching, wrapped in twelve pages of The Times and six pairs of tights, and entombed in a steel-reinforced shoe box, one of Wendy's precious surviving glasses.

I needed to match it, you see. Surely somewhere in London there were identical glasses. Surely I could replace the one I'd smashed without Wendy ever knowing. So what if it cost a bomb in fares? One must maintain good relations with the neighbours. Especially generous and well-endowed ones. (Wendy's well endowed in every sense, actually. In fact, I've often been tempted to dash across and ask her if I could borrow her . . . never mind.)

I first unwrapped Wendy's specimen glass, as reverently as a holy relic, in a very smart, modern glass shop in Marylebone. It was such a smart shop that my mackintosh mysteriously wilted and went spotted as I crossed the threshold. I watched, panting rather coarsely I expect, as the specialist revolved the glass against the light.

'Could be Polish . . .' he murmured. 'Or maybe Scandinavian. Got nothing like it . . . sorry.'

Off I trudged to Shrugge & Smirke, Antique Glass specialist in well-heeled Kensington. I could feel my own heels sinking and breaking out in scuffs as I stood there waiting for the impeccably groomed Catriona Shrugge to deliver her verdict. 'Daifntleh Venetian,' she crooned, 'pahssibly seventeenth centureh. Lairvleh!' But of course she had nothing like it.

In the course of the day I displayed Wendy's glass to fifteen different experts, who told me it was Dutch seventeenth century, English nineteenth century, Finnish twentieth century, French, Italian, Irish and Transylvanian. And of course none of them had anything like it. It could not be matched.

By now, footsore and weary, I had turned into a glasnostic. In future, I vowed, my guests would drink from chipped enamel tooth mugs and jolly well lump it.

I bought Wendy six rather beautiful Swedish glasses as a kind of consolation prize for having broken her glass of great sentimental value. And on the train home I dreaded the horror with which she would receive the news. Would she swoon away at my feet, crying, 'Oh no! My Great Grandmother smuggled them out of occupied Poland in her Liberty Bodice!'?

Trembling, I approached her door, carefully carrying the six new glasses and her remaining five sentimentally valuable ones in a big cardboard carton. Like one of those hard-luck door-to-door salesmen, I set down my burden and told my sad tale. Wendy gasped. Wendy stared. Wendy clapped her hand across her mouth.

'But how ghastly!' she cried. 'I got them at Woolworths!' Just wait till I see Melodramatic Miranda again. I'll have my revenge. And it'll definitely revolve around something I never seem to run out of: ground glass.

Aunt Ursula disapproves of modern foodstuffs

I bought several packets of biscuits. Aunt Ursula is particularly fond of Squashed Flies. She is suspicious about what they put in them now, though I've assured her that it's the same old flies as in the glorious past.

Every first Sunday in the month, my Aunt Ursula visits us in order to denounce modern life. I am often made to feel personally responsible for modern life, even though I only learnt to drive at forty and to this day have no idea what a *management consultant* might be. The night before her last visit, I stayed up until 1am scrubbing the lavatory rim with sandpaper, lest the sight of its stains should provoke from Aunt Ursula a sermon on 'Great Sparkling Toilets of the Past'.

It's a lot easier on the third Sunday in the month, when I take my child to visit her. All I have to do is remove the bubble gum from my daughter's hair and bribe her into Aunt Ursula's latest hot-from-the-1950s child's knitted cardigan. Then off we trot with our basket of groceries, like a couple of Red Riding Hoods off to visit the wolf. Ah, the groceries . . . they're crucial. The idea is to deflect Aunt Ursula's disapproval away from us and onto our hapless foodstuffs. As I wandered up and down the aisles of Safebury's the day before, I tried to choose products of such bizarre modernity, or of such exotic origin, that the wrath of Aunt Ursula would fall like a ton of – well, nothing so vulgarly modern as bricks. Victorian masonry, perhaps.

'What about the Teenage Mutant Hero Spaghetti Shapes, Mummy?' 'Er no, thank you darling, I think that's going a bit too far.' We did not want to provoke an apoplectic seizure in the aged aunt. To placate her I bought several packets of biscuits. Aunt Ursula is particularly fond of Squashed Flies. She is suspicious about what they put in them now, though I've assured her that it's the same old flies as in the glorious past.

When we arrived, she was instantly outraged by the fruit. It was a case of the grapes of wrath. 'You *know* I can't be doing with grape pips, dear,' she warned. 'They get under my plate. And what's this? *Chile?* I daren't touch these hot peppery things, Susan. You Know Why.' 'No, no, Auntie, *Chile:* it's in South America. It's where the grapes come from.' 'I don't hold with things from South America. You don't know where they've been.'

Stifling the desire to suggest that actually we knew exactly where they'd been: Chile, I awaited her next attack. 'We never bothered with this foreign stuff before the War,' she went on, gazing with disbelief at a tin of lychees. 'What's this? Muesli biscuits? I never touch muesli. They're letting them make biscuits out of it, are they? Whatever next?'

She paused to shudder at the thought of what further inroads muesli might make into modern life, and rearranged her skirts as if determined that any encroaching tide of Swiss cereal would not be allowed to rise further than her knees. I enjoyed this moment of peace, but all too soon Aunt Ursula was back in her stride, lamenting the good old pre-War days when her mother regularly fed a family of fourteen on a couple of pig's trotters and a handful of groundsel. 'She could make a sheep's head last a week,' was her grim boast. 'We had to shift for ourselves in those days. Half an oatcake once a month was all the biscuit we ever had – if we were lucky.'

We listened soberly to her celebration of pre-War austerity and accepted her devastating verdict that the range and variety of biscuits – indeed of all groceries – nowadays was but another symptom of moral degeneracy. Then, as usual, she asked me to visit her attic. Alone. Aunt Ursula is haunted by the fear that she has rats in her attic. I privately worry more about the possibility of bats in her belfry, but I always trudge up there obediently ('Your legs are younger than mine!') on a kind of roving rodent patrol.

Resting for a moment by the water tank, as my legs didn't seem to be all that young today, something caught my eye. Lying atop a dusty trunk, faded with age, was ... a dead rat? A live bat? A Rembrandt? No. An Army & Navy Stores Grocery List for 1936. I seized it and opened it at random, 'Bimbo Window & Mirror Powder 5½d a tin,' it read. You've got to admit, it was a great start. And it got better. 'Glitto, Gosp, Gry-moff ... Scourine, Vim, Zog ...'

Zog? I thought he was the ex-King of Albania. It was more than exotic: it was almost extraterrestrial. It was *A Hitch-hiker's Guide To The Groceries* for 1936. I reeled at the sheer range and wonderfulness of the products. And then, recalling Aunt Ursula's absurd tale of only half an oatcake, ever, I turned to the section on biscuits. There were *four pages*: from Moore's Dorset Knobs to Simpson's Thin Captains (these two reminded me of Thomas Hardy) ... from Japanese Mystic Delicacies to French Crêpes Dentelles Gavottes. I ran downstairs flourishing the catalogue and pointed out, in a respectful way, of course, the Puff Cracknells, the Oyster Crackers, the Petticoat Tails and Huntin Nuts. Where, I implied discreetly, was that pre-War austerity we had heard so much about?

Aunt Ursula drew herself up to her full height, always an impressive manoeuvre. She picked up the catalogue and cast an expressive eye over it. Then she sighed with what I can only describe as lyrical nostalgia. 'Ah,' she said. '*Romary's Tunbridge Wells Wafers*. They don't make biscuits like that nowadays.' With a deft flick of the wrist, Aunt Ursula had moved the goal posts and I was face down in the mud. As usual. Nasty, low-quality, modern mud it was too. Still, what can you expect these days?

Trying to survive household hazards

I ran upstairs and threw a whole tubeful of effervescent Vitamin C tablets down the loo. What resulted wasn't so much a Buck's Fizz as an eruption threatening the entire Home Counties.

Just as I thought it was safe to put my head above the parapet, someone lent me *The Urban Survival Handbook*. 'The house has all the ingredients for disaster under one roof: fire, electricity, water, gas, sharp knives, power tools, heights, poisons and chemicals,' warned ex-SAS man John 'Lofty' Wiseman, the author.

'I have watched my seven children growing up,' he continues. Wait! Seven? Evidently there was one area of his life in which Lofty hadn't been all that careful. Still, I set aside my envy of his fertility and tried to concentrate on his life-saving advice.

'Vitamin C Overdose . . .' Impossible, surely? I thought you could take as much Vitamin C as you liked because your body could get rid of any excess. But there are problems, apparently. 'Effervescent tablets often consist largely of sodium bicarbonate and this would be a risk to patients [with] . . . heart or blood pressure problems.'

Now, I wasn't aware of any heart problems, but I had the distinct feeling that I might develop some before I'd finished the book. So I ran upstairs and threw a whole tubeful of effervescent Vitamin C tablets down the loo. What resulted wasn't so much a Buck's Fizz as an eruption threatening the entire Home Counties. I chucked half a pint of Ecover Loo Cleaner down as well, hoping it would act as an antidote. The fizzing grew overpoweringly fragrant. Almost expiring in a cloud of eucalyptus, I seized the book again and read: 'Warning: Don't mix toilet cleaners. In some cases this results in highly toxic fumes which . . . may produce choking and lung irritation.'

After the choking had subsided, I started worrying about

the poor old septic tank. Mr Wiseman warned that if the bacteria in the chambers were killed off by my irresponsibly throwing things down the loo, the whole system could get irrevocably bunged up. Nervously I peered down from the landing window on to the lawn. There were no sinister stains . . . yet. I suppose the whole bunging up could take weeks. Long before then I was going to trip on a toy, suffocate on a plastic bag, or become infested with deathwatch beetle.

The strain of all this was beginning to tell. I needed tea and toast. But wait . . . 'Some toasters can melt dramatically and burst into flames . . .' Instantly I unplugged the toaster (wearing oven gloves to guard against electrocution) and flung it out of the window. Then I flung the oven gloves after it in case they contained asbestos. One of them narrowly missed the postman on his way up the path. But was he the postman? 'Thieves may pose as representatives of gas, water and electricity companies . . . to gain entry . . .'

If only I had a peephole installed! Although peepholes have snags. 'Most peepholes distort the view . . . if the caller is standing too close, they may look frightening.' I stayed in a flat once with a peephole that made every caller look like Orson Welles. And again, 'If you are very short or very tall, the comfortable height for you might not give a good view of the caller.' Shorties like me, in other words, could find themselves trying to judge a caller's intentions by his tummy button. 'If you actually see the tummy button, don't open the door.' That wasn't Lofty, actually, that was me. Good advice, don't you agree? But if there's no tummy button, don't open the door either. It could be an alien.

Bing Bong! Oh no! The bell! I was alone. 'If you are alone, call out and pretend to be talking to someone else. (It may help if the imaginary companion is male.) 'Arnold!' I bawled. 'Mr Schwarzenegger! Could you take the tea through to Mr Tyson and Mr Bruno, please? And ask Lofty Wiseman to tell you about his time in the SAS! I've got to answer the door!'

Bing Bong! The caller was undeterred. I would have to open the door. But first I had to hide my purse. I knew how important it was to Carry Purse In Inside Pocket. I had no inside pocket, but I did have a bra with room for one more on top. Two more, actually. This particular bra dated from the old maternity era and looked as if it was waiting for something to turn up. Deftly I secreted my purse in the left cup. It gave me a square, lopsided look. But no matter: perhaps it would suggest the presence of a secret burglar alarm or a direct line to the local police station.

Composing my features into a horrible scowl, I flung the door open. 'Morning, Sue' said Jim the Postman, with his usual cheery grin. I dropped the scowl – and my purse shot from its hiding place, hit the postman's boots, flew open and scattered small change all over the doorstep. Some of the small 5p pieces were carried away on the wind like seeds, but we managed to corner most of my fortune. The postman handed it to me with a nervous smile – and a parcel – and beat a hasty retreat to his van.

Back indoors, with doors bolted and TV set unplugged, I opened the parcel cautiously. It could be a bomb. But no. It was only the fifty crocus bulbs I'd ordered. And though gardening can be a dangerous pastime, I don't think anyone has ever actually been blown up by a crocus.

I couldn't stand much more of this Urban Survival. Life was too short. I wanted to get back to good old Country Complacency, before all the anxiety gave me a heart attack. I didn't actually throw the book away, though. I keep it by my bed – it's just the right size for braining burglars.

Being a Virgo

It's at this time of year that I'm reminded of an embarrassing little secret. Don't spread it about, but I'm a Virgo. There! Even having to admit it out loud in print makes me cringe. In vain I envy the glamorous Geminis, the sultry Scorpios, the swashbuckling Sagittarians. Not that I believe a word of it, of course. It's all a load of rubbish . . . isn't it?

Being a Virgo puts the horror back in horoscopes. Read any description of us and you'll be instantly repelled. We are cold, analytical, efficient, fanatical, anxious, hypochondriacal, completely uncreative and, worst of all, famously unsexy. Virgospeak is just as bad, revolving as it does around *Good morning. No thank you, How very charming* and *Isn't it time you were thinking of going?*

Now I've always wanted to be a gypsy, with mud on my heels, fire in my eyes and wild romantic whatsit in my blood, despite the fact I'm destined to be the Snow Queen. But listen. If I'm supposed to be the Snow Queen, why is there custard all down my frock? If I'm supposed to be cold, why do I regularly burst into tears when I see those ads with old Fred or Bert – the gardener who's nearly past it? If I'm fastidious and efficient, why is there a boiled sweet on my shoe? If I'm uncreative and hygienic, why have I earned my living for the past ten years by spinning yarns and cracking slightly below-the-belt jokes? If I'm unsexy . . . well, all right, I admit there might be something in this Virgo business.

But this year I decided to cock a snook at my Zodiac destiny. That in itself proves I'm not a Virgo, doesn't it? No Virgo would be seen dead cocking a snook. It would be fatal to their dignity. And as for my Virgoan dignity, well, I did have some once, but I can't for the life of me think where I could have left it. On the bus, probably. And that's another thing. No Virgo would ever run for the bus, as I do, regularly, and miss it. Virgos are all chillingly purposeful cyclists. I was a cyclist when I lived in London, but I wasn't chillingly purposeful. Most of the time I had oil all over my hands, head between my spokes and bum in the air.

Anyway. To cock a snook at the whole idea of Virgos, I was going to spend an entire day being wild and gypsyish and creative all over the place. I wasn't sure if I could quite rise to the challenge of being red-hot and sexy, but I was going to be warm, dammit. Or tepid at least. As long as I could wear my thermal vest.

I started well. I lay in bed for five minutes, sipping a glass of de-alcoholised wine and painting my toenails passionate pink. When my daughter came in to say good morning, instead of me snapping *Get dressed at once, No you may not watch telly, Hurry up or we'll be late* . . . I grabbed her, pulled her into bed with me and covered her with big sloppy kisses to show her just how cold and undemonstrative I wasn't.

'For goodness' sake, Mummy, let go!' She struggled from my gypsyish embrace. 'Can I watch telly?'

'Of course, darling,' I gushed in a warm, creative way. 'Whatever you want.'

I thought I'd have a little lie-in myself for once: listen to the *Today* programme, leave the laundry for later (only in the interests of my experiment, you understand: to demonstrate the fallacy of astrology). I reached out to switch on my radio and knocked over a tumbler full of water. I watched as it performed a graceful somersault and deposited all the liquid into my open handbag.

I gave an exaggerated shrug and studied with interest the puddles forming in and around my bag. So what if its entire contents were soaked? It was only my passport, bankbook, address book, diary and £60 in cash – the mere debris of civilisation. In the grand planetary scheme of things, my handbag was laughably trivial.

Suddenly the phone rang. I lurched bolt upright and grabbed it. Old habits die hard. 'Mrs Limb?' came a polite voice from the other end of the line. It was too polite, actually. Definitely a Virgo.

'I've got some people who'd like to see the house,' said the Virgo-spy masquerading as an Estate Agent, 'Would 10am be convenient?'

Yes, my house is on the market – but never mind about the details of all that, now. I shot from my bed like a guided missile, washed, dried and folded my daughter, deposited her, still crackling, at school, drove back home like a bat out of hell (a sensible and prudent bat, of course), and attacked the house.

Its carpets were combed, its cushions thrashed, two tons of miscellaneous junk were swept under the beds, the kitchen floor was scalded and the ceilings tweaked with a feather duster. By the time I'd finished, even the tassels on the cords that hold back the curtains had been washed, conditioned, and had had their split ends trimmed. And even then, one strand wasn't hanging quite straight. It bothered me for weeks.

The prospective vendors didn't like the house, but I was glad. I could see at a glance they were sexy Sagittarians. I wouldn't want people like that taking over my gleaming tiles anyway. Being swashbuckling and creative and stuff all over my nice clean floor. Ugh!

Well, I'm afraid that you must excuse me now, but it's time I was going. I've still got to Hoover the cat, dust the garage and iron the doormat.